Royals

It's th

Breaking news: newly crowned King Sebastian and reformed rebel Prince Alessio are headed to the altar. They're short just one thing—a bride!

Determined to redeem his scandalous past and prove he's worthy of his title, Alessio promises to rejuvenate Celiana's tourism with a bride lottery. And the lucky winner will become his princess!

Brie never expected to win. Her name was only in the running as a publicity stunt to promote her fledgeling marketing business. Now she's engaged to a prince and #lottobride is trending!

From birth, Sebastian was destined to take the throne. But being perfect never earned him the love he craved. Now he'll commit himself to a life of duty only, which means a marriage of convenience with local aristocrat Lady Breanna...

Breanna has always put everyone else's happiness ahead of her own. Yet her unexpected chemistry with Sebastian makes her wish their fairy-tale royal wedding could be for more than just the cameras...

Find out what happens behind palace doors in Juliette Hyland's debut for Harlequin Romance!

Prince Alessio and Brie's story
How to Win a Prince
Available now!

King Sebastian and Lady Breanna's story
Coming soon!

Dear Reader,

Every writer has a few stories "under the bed." The early stories, the rough starts, the things we loved but went nowhere. Five years ago, I thought up a princess lottery. I wrote a few chapters...not great. I tried again a year later—still not ready. But last year, I pulled Brie and Alessio back out, gave it one more shot and *How to Win a Prince* was born.

Brie Ailiono grew up in privilege, until she refused to accept the groom her family handpicked. Tossed out with nothing, she's determined to run her marketing business and live life by her own rules. The only catch: Prince Alessio pulling her name out in the Princess Lottery.

Prince Alessio was the rebel who hated every second of royal life. But he owes his brother, the new king. So he'll do his duty and reignite the kingdom's place as the honeymoon capital of the world with his own "love story." The only problem: the winner doesn't want the crown. Can he show Brie that she really wants to win a prince?

Juliette Hyland

How to Win a Prince

—

Juliette Hyland

Recycling programs
for this product may
not exist in your area.

ISBN-13: 978-1-335-59651-2

How to Win a Prince

Harlequin Enterprises ULC
22 Adelaide St. West, 41st Floor
Toronto, Ontario M5H 4E3, Canada
www.Harlequin.com

Printed in U.S.A.

Juliette Hyland believes in strong coffee, hot drinks and happily-ever-afters! She lives in Ohio, USA, with her prince charming, who has patiently listened to many rants regarding characters failing to follow the outline. When not working on fun and flirty happily-ever-afters, Juliette can be found spending time with her beautiful daughters, giant dogs or sewing uneven stitches with her sewing machine.

Books by Juliette Hyland

Harlequin Medical Romance

Boston Christmas Miracles

A Puppy on the 34th Ward

Neonatal Nurses

A Nurse to Claim His Heart

The Pediatrician's Twin Bombshell
Reawakened at the South Pole
The Vet's Unexpected Houseguest
The Prince's One-Night Baby
Rules of Their Fake Florida Fling
Redeeming Her Hot-Shot Vet
Tempted by Her Royal Best Friend

Visit the Author Profile page
at Harlequin.com.

For my editor, Laurie, who helped take this
long-held story dream and make it a reality!

Praise for
Juliette Hyland

"A delightful second chance on love with intriguing
characters, powerful back stories and tantalizing
chemistry! Juliette Hyland quickly catches her
reader's attention.... I really enjoyed their story! I
highly recommend this book.... The story line has a
medical setting with a whole lot of feels in the mix!"

—*Goodreads* on *Falling Again for the Single Dad*

CHAPTER ONE

BRIELLA AILIONO SNAPPED another photo of herself, hoping the angle highlighted the long dark gown her best friend had designed for this final engagement. The image was about the dress, not her, but if she'd learned anything, it was that appearances were always scrutinized. If her mother was still talking to her, Brie might thank her for the multitude of lessons she'd taught on the subject.

She scrunched her nose as she examined the image. She wasn't as bubbly as the other potential brides here, wasn't bouncy and excited for the tiny possibility she'd win the "prize" in a few minutes. She only had one princess ticket in the giant glass spinning lotto wheel up on the palace's balcony. One shot to become a princess. One shot to wear a crown.

One shot too many!

Prince Alessio's Princess Lottery was all the country of Celiana had talked about for the last year. Throughout each week, potential brides had purchased tickets and then deposited them on Sunday while cameras watched. It was a year of spectacle.

If she could have devised any other way to launch Ophelia's bridal gown and specialty dress shop so quickly, Brie would have. A standard rollout with a mixture of graphics across social media platforms, booths at bridal fairs, a well-placed billboard or sponsored "news article" were options.

Success lay down that path, in two or three years. This way, this scheme, with her standing next to all the brides in a new wedding dress designed by Ophelia as she rattled off comments about the gown and the spectacle... Well, it meant success was at Ophelia's door year one. And wild success, too, not just keep-the-doors-open, scrape-by success.

And her own business was rocketing out of the gate, too.

Her marketing firm; her "little" business, the one her parents refused to acknowledge—it had a phone that never stopped ringing. An overflowing email inbox. Even buyout offers. There were possibilities at every corner.

Built from the ground up with no help from her family, it was Brie's achievement. All hers. She was making the choices—finally in charge of her own life.

The cost was a ticket in the Princess Lottery. The winner got a crown, and Prince Alessio as a husband.

Blowing out a breath, she looked at the image on her phone. It was good, and the dark dress was highlighted nicely against the wall of white and cream behind her. She stood out.

Which was the point of this marketing campaign.

"If my name comes out, I think I might just faint!"

"Me too!" the women squealed, then looked at Brie.

She raised a hand and winked as their eyes widened. Her dress's dark hue gave off a less hopeful vibe. Though like all Ophelia's designs, it was gorgeous.

"Good luck, ladies." Brie smiled as they walked away. She didn't really mean the words. No one should "win" their groom.

But the palace hadn't asked her thoughts on this marketing campaign. If they had, she'd have at least pointed out that requiring attendance on the palace grounds, if you'd placed your name in the lottery, was a terrible plan. There was exactly one lucky winner, and over a hundred unhappy losers.

Not great optics, which was unusual for an entity whose whole role one could label "optics."

"This is so exciting! So exciting!" The squeals echoed behind her.

It felt like she was the lone person here who didn't want to wear a crown.

You are!

If she didn't need to be here for the final splash of Ophelia's wedding dress line, she'd have watched this play out on her small television screen in yoga pants, a T-shirt, messy bun and with a giant bowl of popcorn.

Instead, she was the standout in a sea of princess hopefuls dressed in bright cream.

"If my name comes out of that monstrosity, I suspect I'll do more than faint," she murmured, keeping her eye on the balcony where Prince Alessio would appear any minute.

"Not excited about the possibility of becoming a princess?" Nate, one of the local reporters who hadn't gotten the plum press pass the palace gave international media, asked as he sidled up next to her. "People consider Prince Alessio the most handsome prince."

There is one prince in this country—not much of a competition.

Though even before his brother, Sebastian, was crowned king, Alessio would have won that title. The spare had become the superhot heir.

Whoever ended up with Alessio would never have a hard time looking at him. He was tall and blond with brilliant green eyes, muscular shoulders and full lips. The handsome prince was not the issue she had with this public relations stunt.

The palace swore the reformed rebel was excited for this. The man who'd left Celiana for almost three years, only returning following his father's stroke, was happy. That was the story they needed. Easier to sell to the masses.

The real story was about ledgers. This modern fairy tale was the quickest way to remind the world that Celiana was once the honeymoon capital of Europe. It had already boosted the country's tourism and aided shops and attractions struggling since the global tourism economy crashed a few years ago.

In each press release and interview, Alessio dutifully discussed the woman he'd meet at the altar as though he already loved her—like that was even possible. He reminded everyone that his parents had had a marriage of convenience that turned to a great love. Then he worked back to the benefits for the country, reminding anyone watching that Celiana was the most romantic place to start your union.

A bride to right the country's travel economy… who wouldn't want to fill that role?

She couldn't fault Alessio for caring about the people of this country. Their elected leaders were more concerned with retaining power. And Alessio seemed far more concerned with the kingdom's day-to-day running than his brother.

The once dutiful Prince Sebastian, now King, was missing engagements and generally acting like a playboy, and the previously rebellious spare was stepping in for the benefit of Celiana. The role reversal for the men since their father passed was an epic story.

Or it would be, if the palace commented on it.

There were other ways, better options, to jumpstart the tourism industry.

"My dreams don't involve a crown."

Her dreams had already cost her the aristocratic life she'd been born into. Cost her the family that "loved" her only when she performed the script they'd drafted from the moment of her birth. She wanted to be more than a trophy wife to some man her father wanted to do business with. She was carving her own path.

Brie's dreams were going to carry her from the small, rented office to a penthouse with a view. No one else was writing the story of her life. Nope. Briella Ailiono controlled all her publicity statements—not that she actually planned to make any about her personal life.

"Since my name is only in there once, the odds are very good I will have to fight with everyone else for a place on public transportation following this fiasco."

She shook her head and looked to the balcony again.

Where was Alessio?

He was meant to pick his bride at the top of the hour, and it was three minutes past. Maybe he was having second thoughts.

Marriage was a commitment, one that should involve love. A promise of forever between two people who cared for each other, rooted each other on.

The opposite of her parents' union.

Her best friend, Ophelia, and her husband, Rafael, had the kind of union Brie would have.

If she ever met someone at the altar.

After watching them cheer each other on, love one another in sickness, health and business ventures, she would not settle for less.

She'd spent her teen years surrounded by people who only cared about her family's wealth. It was better to be alone than to marry for power and connections.

"Care to make a comment for the press?" Nate grinned as he held up his notebook.

There were many comments she wanted to make. She wanted to call this whole thing out for what it was: a PR stunt that made the heir to the throne a prize for whoever's name got picked. The prince was a commodity instead of a man worthy of having a partner who chose him.

And it wasn't like this was a true game of chance. The lottery had gone on all year, with the press corps gleefully showing up weekly to watch women put the tickets they'd purchased into the huge crystal ball specially made for this occasion.

Each "bride" could put her name in once a week for fifty-two weeks. The first week the entry was free…a stunt to show that anyone could be the next princess of Celiana—and the reason more than a thousand women had entered the first week.

But with each week, the cost of entry rose by ten euros—donated to the arts fund Prince Alessio championed. It was a good cause, but the price was steep for a year's worth of tickets. Thirteen thousand euros was needed for a genuine chance at the crown.

That meant there were very few women who could expect to step onto the balcony today. All were from wealthy families. In fact, the final week

Brie had watched less than twenty women put their names in. Those were the ones most likely to stand on Alessio's arm today. All "real" princess material.

"No one wants to hear my thoughts on this, Nate."

"It's just as well," the reporter huffed. "I doubt anything I write will make the cut anyway. The actual story is the women up there." He pointed to the front of the group—where those with fifty-two entries stood.

"So true. They look beautiful. Several are wearing Ophelia's gowns."

She grinned as she looked to Anastasia and Breanna. She'd been in the same class in school as the identical twins, though not close friends. Even as girls, their parents had made little secret of their plan to marry their daughters to the crown. Her parents had thought the plan to marry Breanna to Alessio and Anastasia to Sebastian was crass and had discouraged Brie from forming any close attachment.

It was horrible of her parents, though when the twins' mother had mentioned being fine about interchanging the girls if one was pulled as the lotto bride, Brie had cringed. The words were horrible, and the fact that the girls were picking bridal outfits for today made it so much worse.

Not that the twins had reacted. Neither had commented as Ophelia fitted them. Their silence broke Brie's heart. They deserved more than a scheming family. But the price of breaking with your powerful family, the price Brie had paid, was high. She couldn't judge others for not choosing it.

"The wedding gown thing is weird." Nate chuckled as he looked at the women all around. "It's not like the marriage is happening today."

"Agreed."

She looked at the sea of white. The contract they'd all signed when entering this fiasco had required their attendance today and the wearing of a gown fit for a bride. What were women supposed to do with the gowns after today?

It was unlikely they'd want to wear them when they met their true love, but she supposed the royal family didn't think of such minor details.

"Black is an interesting choice."

This she was willing to put on the record. "You can print this. My dress is technically dark green, Nate." She held up the small train, letting the light hit it just right. "At Ophelia's there is a wide variety of gowns, including a selection of dresses with a modern flair."

"It certainly stands out. Though I'm not sure my editor will print that."

The green stood out. That was the purpose, but it was also her own personal statement.

"Dark colors are best when love dies."

"Ouch!" Nate bent over, pretending to take the hit to the gut, then laughed. "Guess you won't cry if your name doesn't come out today."

"I'll cry if it does!"

The last thing she wanted was a marriage of convenience, particularly one trying to save the kingdom. That was too much pressure. It was a burden even the now-dutiful prince shouldn't have on his shoulders.

"The prince!"

The cry went up from the gathered and Brie took another photo. The whole point of this was to make Ophelia's shop shine.

Going live on her social media site, Brie waved and smiled as people started joining the live stream. Sure, the national and international media were here, but Brie was an actual potential bride who'd been at the crystal entry ball every week this year. Her following had reached two million last week as people waited for today's outcome.

"Prince Alessio just stepped to the balcony. He's wearing a dark suit…"

Mourning the loss of love for himself?

Brie didn't know why that thought bothered her. After all, he seemed the ever-willing participant in this game.

She was too far away to see his face, but his walk seemed stilted. It was a hitch that she wasn't sure the cheering crowd noticed.

"We offer a wide range of suits for the suit lover in your life, too." Brie's voice was bright as she flipped the screen back to her. "He's reaching into the vat of tickets! Who will be our new princess?"

Cries of excitement echoed around her as she waved for the camera. This was finally almost over, and she'd done a good job. Ophelia's shop was on the international market now. Her appointment books were full for the next six months! Brie's baby company was entering the international stage, too.

It meant the Ailiono family would never control her life again.

"Briella Ailiono." The call echoed across the field.

Time slowed as she watched the phone fall from her fingers. No. No. *No.*

"Briella Ailiono!" Alessio called again, hoping his voice sounded steady. Every bit of today would be monitored, filmed, dissected. Those looking for a love story would swoon; those thinking this was nothing more than a charade would look for any sign that Alessio wasn't sure of the plan.

He was sure…sure that this plan would revive Celiana's wedding and honeymoon tourism industry. He was certain that the people would benefit from it, and equally certain that he owed his father's memory more than being known as the rebellious prince who'd fought with him just before the stroke that ultimately stole him away.

Marriages of convenience were the way of the royal life. And there were benefits to wearing a crown… Hopefully they outweighed the thorns for Briella.

Where was his bride? Shouldn't she be running to the front…brimming with excitement?

He knew she was here; attendance at the lottery was mandatory.

In a wedding dress.

That was an instance of dark humor gone wrong. From his brother, King Sebastian, whose word was now taken far more seriously. He was a man Alessio hadn't thought capable of cracking a joke before their father died. But Sebastian wasn't the same since the crown of Celiana had landed on his head. The dutiful son, the heir to the throne, the one who'd always known his place in the family, seemed lost as destiny finally gave him what he'd been trained for.

And that left Alessio in the role of dutiful heir. It was not a position he coveted…but if not for his fight, his rebellion, perhaps his father's blood pressure wouldn't have spiked. Maybe this wasn't the role Alessio wanted, but it was the one he owed.

"Where is she?" Alessio looked over the balcony. The crowd was dispersing, and no one looked like the happy winner.

"She was live on her social media page just as you called her name," his mother, Genevieve, said. The queen mother offered an encouraging smile, something he'd rarely seen in private after his father's untimely death.

Not that Queen Genevieve had ever smiled much. The love story between King Cedric and his queen was well scripted. Everything about it perpetuated the island's fairy tale. But like most fairy tales, the proper story lacked luster.

His mother and father had never loved each other. They respected one another, but it wasn't love. Alessio doubted his father was capable of loving anything besides the country he'd served.

It was King Cedric who'd mentioned how well the island flourished after his union with Queen Genevieve. His father had contacted Alessio, asking him to marry. That was in the "before times," when he was in his little glass shop in Scotland, working, acting, as just a man. It was the happiest he'd ever been.

His father had told him he owed it to the people of Celiana. Alessio had countered that he didn't owe anyone anything, that the future king should do it.

King Cedric said no one would believe a queen lottery. That as the heir the expectations for Sebastian were different. His father was looking for a foreign match, one worthy of the title of queen. Alessio's match was far less important since he'd never sit on the throne. It was a pointed reminder that Alessio was second in his father's eyes, heart and plans—in all things.

They'd screamed at each other. He'd said some terrible things. Things he couldn't take back now.

His father's stroke happened less than an hour after Alessio hung up the phone. The king had never regained consciousness. He'd never realized Alessio had returned home, embraced his father's plans and followed through. This world was his prison, but he would do his best to make sure Briella was content.

Somehow.

At least the stunt was working. The shops were busy. The island's hotels and hostels were booked solid. Many of the residents had opened their guest bedrooms for people wanting to visit…for a fee.

His father's final idea was saving Celiana.

And nearly a year of wedding planning would cement the country's place again.

Celiana—the home of your love story.

Becoming engaged to a stranger was unnerving. There was no way to sugarcoat that. However, for centuries royals had signed documents, wed strangers and then spent years betrothed. At least he and Briella had time to get to know each other before setting an actual date. His lottery was unique, but the idea of a union for business or the greater good of a country was ancient.

That reminder did little to calm his racing nerves as he looked over the departing crowd. There was still no sign of Briella.

He knew her. Or rather, knew *of* her as the outcast of the Ailiono family. They owned more land than anyone else on the island. Their businesses touched nearly every aspect of life on Celiana. Not that they'd done much to help the country. The family only focused on adding to their already endless coffers.

And their daughter had done something to get disowned, something they refused to discuss. He didn't understand why she would willingly step back into this world, but maybe she'd not wanted to leave. Most aristocrats clung to power, hating even the thought that they might lose the thing they felt made them better than others.

Ridiculous.

"Her live ended as soon as you said her name." His mother's words pulled his mind away from his worries—mostly.

"Live?" He looked over the departing sea of white, again trying to imagine where Briella was and why she wasn't racing to where the royal guard was waiting for her.

"She's the marketing manager for a dress shop. She's stunning and she talks about the shop, highlighting why one should get their wedding day attire from Ophelia's. It's a brilliant campaign."

That his mother would know that was only a little surprising. Through social media, she'd followed the eighteen brides with fifty-two entries as closely as Alessio had followed the economic progress. She was in her own way vetting potential daughters-in-law. If Briella was marketing through the lotto, the queen mother would have seen her.

"Your father would have enjoyed the ingenuity. That was something he respected." The queen mother tipped her head, looking at the departing "brides."

He thought his mother missed his father, but it was like one missed a confidant, not a great love. Stepping away from the balcony, he patted her arm. Affection was not something the royal family did well.

"He'd have been proud of you focusing on Celiana's future."

No, he wouldn't.

Alessio was doing what was expected of him. That did not earn a place of pride in the royal family. His father gave everything to Celiana. Doing anything less than that was unacceptable, even if the palace walls felt like they were always closing in.

"I know he thought a royal wedding was a good idea. Ours worked...mostly." She bit her lip and offered a smile, but there was something in her voice. The unstated hesitancy sent his stomach spinning.

Briella would have adjustments to make. Life as a royal was not the glamorous stuff of magazines or the fantasy of movies. The royals of Celiana served the country and its people. The sacrifices that came with that—well, the sacrifices of a few for the many—were the bedrock of royal service. He'd run from his duties once, but not again.

"This way, Princess."

"I am not a princess." Her tone was sharp, carrying around the corner as security led her to him.

His stomach, already unsettled from the day's activities, tumbled on the sound. She didn't sound happy or excited. He'd counted on the winner being thrilled, happily standing beside him for the rest of the day's activities with a giant smile. The blushing bride-to-be. He'd selfishly even hoped her excitement would quell his anxiety that had grown stronger as today crept ever closer on the calendar.

They needed to present a united front. It was necessary to quiet the naysayers, who claimed this was nothing more than a short-term publicity stunt.

There were whispers floating through social media and a few regular news channels. The rumors, if proved true, could impact the entire country. A royal wedding brought tourism and prosperity. A royal scandal... That could undo everything.

"She was trying to flee," Henri, head of security, stated as he deposited Briella in the small alcove.

Flee?

"A runaway bride... That is quite the headline.

Though not the one we're aiming for," Alessio quipped as he stepped forward.

Briella let out a soft chuckle as her bright blue eyes met his. She was gorgeous; her long blond hair was wrapped in an intricate braid, and a near-black dress hugged her curves in all the right places.

The few times he'd seen her at court, she'd been reserved. Not a slip of laughter or hair out of place, she was the perfect Ailiono daughter. Until she wasn't. Rumors swirled about the reasons, but there'd been no concrete answers.

"Running away would be easier in tennis shoes… I might have even made it." She glared at the fancy heels poking out from under the gorgeous dress.

"One often overlooks the power of footwear." Alessio shrugged, not quite sure what to make of this conversation. The idea of running was intoxicating. During the three years he'd lived abroad, he'd felt freer than he ever expected to feel again.

"I should have considered it, apparently." She crossed her arms as her ice-blue eyes caught his.

Any words he might say evaporated as he met her gaze. He'd planned to bow to his bride-to-be, exchange a few pleasantries, bask in her excitement. He'd focus on the spectacle as he tried to make it through the next steps.

Now…now he couldn't quite find any kind of response.

Briella bit her lip then shook herself. "My apologies, Your Majesties... Your Highness." Dipping into a low curtsy, she let out a soft noise he feared was a caught sob.

That broke his heart. He might not be sure of this plan, but there were no monsters in this castle. Well, not really.

"Mother, could you give Briella and me a few minutes?"

The queen mother looked at Briella, still bent in her curtsy, and nodded. "I'll have the king delay the formal announcement and pictures a few minutes."

It was still weird to think of Sebastian as the king.

"Thank you." He slid down to the ground, catching the shock of surprise in Briella's face before she smoothed it over and joined him on the floor.

That was an ability the royal family excelled at, too. He instantly recognized the ability to conceal all feelings. And he hated that she'd learned the trick. Hated that she was using it on him.

Why wouldn't she?

"Briella—" He crossed his legs and leaned forward, making it clear that he was paying attention but giving her a little space.

"Brie." She coughed, clearing the sobs from her throat as she looked at him. "I prefer Brie. We're sitting like kids in a gym class."

"It's comfortable." Honestly, he'd sat without thinking. The position was hardly regal.

It was something he'd once have done to anger his father.

"Though before we go out, I'll have to ask you to look at my pants and make sure I have no dust on them. Pictures and all…we wouldn't want dust to take center stage in today's narrative."

"Of course not." Brie shook her head. "Dust is such an important factor for the press."

"Royalty is all about the show."

It was the first lesson princes and princesses learned. Everything is documented, speculated on, gossiped over.

"What the heck is this conversation?" Brie put her fingers on her forehead, rubbing at the line between her brows.

"The first lesson in your new life. Things that seem meaningless matter."

"This isn't a life I want."

Her cheeks darkened as she rolled her eyes. Her voice was soft, but the hint of terror came through clearly. He reached across and took her hand, squeezing it, trying to ground her.

Grounding himself.

It wasn't one he wanted, either, but that hardly mattered. She'd signed a contract. For all legal matters, she was basically a princess.

Her hand in his was warm. It felt…right? That was a weird descriptor; after all, they didn't know each other. Not really. She was to be his bride, but today, today was an unknown.

"Brie."

He offered what he hoped was a comforting smile as she broke the connection between them. The empty feeling in his palm echoed through his soul. He wanted to reach back out to her.

If you didn't want this, you shouldn't have put your name in the contest.

Saying those words wouldn't help now.

"Brie," he started over. "We have guests we need to see to. Expectations to meet."

"Expectations."

She propped her hands on her knees. In another time or place, they might have been sitting in the schoolyard waiting for their turn on the tennis or basketball court. Instead, they were in fancy clothes on the floor of his father's office—a room his brother still refused to convert to his.

"How can you possibly think of expectations? We don't even know each other. What, we just go out and role-play happily-ever-after?"

Role-playing was the name of the game. Hell, he'd expected his bride to be so excited. That way people might not notice his own discomfort. Instead, he was trying to convince her to go along with the day's duty.

"We have our whole lives to get to know one another." Not exactly comforting, but true.

"Our whole lives!" Brie stood, her dress swooshing with the quick movement. She walked past him and started pacing. "Our whole lives, Your Royal Highness—"

"Alessio," he interrupted as he stood. "It is only right that you call me by my first name, too. At least in private."

"In private. This can't be happening."

He'd felt the same many times. Yet it didn't change what had to be done. "But it is."

"I don't want to marry you." Brie planted her feet, preparing for battle.

This was not in the day's script. His mind raced; what was he supposed to say to that? The rebel buried in his soul shouted with joy before he reminded himself to keep calm. Duty was his life now.

Alessio sucked in a deep breath. That bought him seconds but didn't stop the pounding of his heartbeat in his ears. He'd spent a year figuring out how to make his father's goal a reality—a royal wedding for the country to rally around. Then another year prepping for today. It couldn't unravel. It simply couldn't.

There was no other plan. If this imploded today, Celiana's name would be in papers globally for days, maybe weeks.

For all the wrong reasons.

He could already see the headline: Princess Lottery Bust!

The success Celiana had gained would evaporate overnight. And coming home after his father's stroke, taking up the mantle of duty he'd sworn off, being the face of Celiana's resurgence…it would all have been for nothing. That couldn't happen.

"If you didn't want to be a princess, why was your name in the lottery?"

It wasn't like they'd forced people to put their names in. It was a choice. One that more than a thousand women had chosen.

She'd chosen this…just like he had. And with that came a responsibility to the people depending on them.

"To help Ophelia!" Brie rocked back on her feet as she looked toward the balcony. "To help her get her wedding dress business off the ground. It was a marketing stunt to help my friend. My name was in there once.

"Once," she whispered the word again.

One lucky ticket was what the lottery was all about. He'd parroted that line in many interviews. Alessio hadn't actually counted on someone with one free entry winning. But her reasoning was perfect.

Dutiful…but in a different way.

"That was kind of you." Alessio stepped to her side, grateful when she didn't step away. Helping her friend was admirable. And it was what she'd be doing as a princess.

Except instead of one friend, she'd help the entire kingdom.

"Kind?" Brie's sapphire gaze met his. "It was a marketing strategy, Alessio." Her body shifted and for a moment, he thought she might lean toward him.

"So is the lottery. A marketing strategy to jumpstart the tourism industry. One that is working."

"And the only cost is *our* futures."

A tear slipped down her cheek and his hand rose without him thinking. His thumb rubbed away the drop, and Brie let out a sigh as he cupped her face.

"You signed a contract. Duty is why you put your name in. Duty is why you continue. We'll make it work."

"Make it work." Brie's hand rose, taking his and pulling it away from her face. She squeezed his fingers, her mouth opening as her eyes darted to their joined hands, before she let him go. "Make it work… Such romantic words."

Romance wasn't in the cards. The *idea* of romance was…but *actual* romance? That was not what royal marriages really were.

"According to the movies, Prince Charming and his bride always live happily ever after."

He wasn't Prince Charming. That ideal didn't exist. At least Brie knew that already. He wouldn't have to watch the light dim from his lottery bride as the realization struck.

"This isn't a joke."

The old Alessio would have said that this whole thing was a joke, a giant prank that was over-the-top. Unfortunately, the die was cast.

"You're right," Alessio agreed. "It's our duty to Celiana."

Brie looked at the door. Voices were mixing on the other side of it. A host of events was scheduled for today.

"What if I make you a deal?"

"A deal?" He needed to shut this down, they needed to get moving…but curiosity, and a hint of the rebel he'd been, kept him in place.

"Yes. This was a publicity stunt, and I am a marketing manager now. What if I can get tourism moving in areas not revolving around this? In six to eight weeks, if the focus is on something besides just us, we part ways."

"How would we even measure that?" As the question fell from his lips, he realized there was hope in it, hope that she might actually know a way. Hope he couldn't afford.

"The same way any business measures success." Brie rolled her eyes, gesturing into the air at nothing. Her thoughts on the Princess Lottery were quite clear. "We measure hotel bookings. The bookings need to increase in the next eight weeks—let's say by at least five percent—and tourism at our major sites needs a ten percent bump. That is doable in eight weeks or less."

Was it doable? If so... No. He needed to shut this down now.

"The contract for entry was binding. We've entered into a royal marriage contract and there's no going back."

The contract was similar to the one his parents had signed.

"I'm aware of what I signed. But if the royal family finds me an inappropriate match, you can void the contract."

She'd read the fine print.

"If I show you that I can get the tourism industry back to what it was without the need for a royal wedding, then you can find me inappropriate and end the contract."

The word *no* was on the tip of his tongue, and he knew that was the right answer, but the idea of fulfilling his end of this devil's bargain, while not having to go through with a royal wedding... It was intoxicating.

What if he could make good on the argument he'd had the night his father died without giving up everything?

But what did that mean for Celiana? If the tourists didn't come back for the royal wedding, would they come back at all?

"What if I convince you that there are benefits to royal life? That yes, the trade-off can be steep, but you can find rewarding things in service?"

Those dutiful words had been parroted so often

to him when he'd complained that he'd had no choice in the position of his birth. They were the words he should have said immediately when she offered the deal.

"So rewarding you ran away."

Touché.

"I came back."

She raised an eyebrow and shifted, like she wanted to call out the statement, poke at it.

"I can show you another way. A better way." Brie crossed her arms.

He saw so much of the man he used to be in her. Trapping that energy felt wrong, but duty still came first. It had to…didn't it?

"Without a scandal that destroys the kingdom or my brother's reign." His fight had led to so much damage already; he would not add to it. He couldn't.

Brie bit her lip before nodding. "If we can't do it without those things, then I guess I meet you at the altar." She held out a hand. "Deal?"

"Deal." For the first time since returning to Celiana, Alessio thought there might be a way to earn his freedom. Maybe.

"All right, first steps." She pulled out her phone and took a deep breath. "Do I look like I've been crying?"

"No. Your cheeks are a little flushed, but that's all. Why?"

"We have to tell our followers what we're doing.

Rule one of marketing, don't miss prime opportunities. And flushed works. People can think you swept me off my feet."

She held up her phone and looked at him.

"Do you blush when you're swept off your feet?" he asked.

"No one's ever tried."

That was a shame. A woman who stepped in for a friend, who was so determined to chart her own course, deserved someone who'd sweep her off her feet. If her plan worked, then she'd get that chance.

Why did that give him an uncomfortable feeling?

"All right, Prince Charming, here we go." She pressed a few buttons. "Smile!"

He wasn't sure if the order was for him or her.

"Surprise!" She waved at the camera. "Guess who's here with me."

Brie stepped beside him, and he wrapped a hand around her waist. Her hip brushed his, but she didn't remove his hand.

"I guess you all get to follow me on my path to being a princess now!" Her voice was too bright. Too happy. "It's going to be a blast." She waved and disconnected the live.

"We'll get better." Brie blew out a breath as she glared at the phone.

"I thought that was fine."

She stepped away, just out of arm's reach. "That's

why I'm the marketing manager. We came off stilted. *I* came off stilted. I'll make a post later about nerves and seeing royalty. It will be okay."

He suspected the *It will be okay* was meant for herself. Still, it was time for the next stage.

"We can practice with the guests here." He offered her his hand.

"Right." Brie slid her hand into his.

She looked up at him. Her full pink lips were so close, so perfect. Her hips shifted, pressing against him. It was an odd moment, one that his former self would enjoy too much. The old Alessio might even have joked that one sealed such deals with kisses.

Kissing Brie… His mind tumbled through the thoughts as the air in the room seemed to guide them together.

The crowd let out a cheer on the other side of the study door, breaking whatever magic was spinning between them.

Brie breathed out. "Ready or not."

"Ready or not." Alessio squeezed her hand, grateful that it was this woman standing beside him. Grateful that fate might have given him another chance at freedom.

CHAPTER TWO

How had the day gone so off course? She was meant to be home, not reminding herself to not flinch as camera flashes popped off. Brie's feet were ice blocks, and the idea that she had to step into the room, pretend to be a happy princess-to-be, made her stomach twist. This wasn't the plan.

This evening was supposed to be about celebrating Ophelia's successes and planning the next steps of her future. She needed to focus, find the next steps. That was what Brie did well.

Yes, she was standing next to Alessio. After making a deal with him and nearly kissing him. Kissing… Her mind wanted to wander back to that moment. Even with all the calls and camera flashes, it was that moment her brain wanted to replay. He'd nearly kissed her.

At least she thought he was going to kiss her. Brie had very little experience with that. Well, none actually. She'd not lied when she told Alessio no one had ever tried to sweep her off her feet.

Her family had kept her sheltered, which was a fancy word for controlled her. The few men who'd asked her out after her escape had wanted access to the Ailiono family. She'd gone on exactly three second dates and no third.

The romance books she devoured described the moment before lips connected. The light touch of his fingers. The scent of sandalwood and cedar. The hesitation and excitement.

All those things were present. Except Alessio smelled like the ocean, fresh and free.

The prince, who'd joked about shoes and runaway brides, was rigid now. It was the dutiful Alessio beside her. The one who'd returned from overseas, never discussing what he'd done, assuming the burden of expectation.

Except she'd seen the hint of resignation in his eyes. It was a look she'd worn so often in her family's home. It was that look that made her ask for the deal, which he'd agreed to far quicker than she'd expected.

Maybe he acted like the dutiful prince, but she thought the rebel was still there. He yearned for freedom as much as she did.

Alessio leaned his head against hers. "Take a breath, Brie." The words were barely audible, but his arm slipped around her waist.

Her lungs screamed as she inhaled fresh oxygen.

"It's role-playing, remember."

His soft voice insinuated itself to her soul, reminding her of what was at stake. They needed to look happy today. In a few weeks, they could start pulling away in preparation for ending the engagement, but today... Today they needed to look happy.

His fingers gripped her waist, comfort washing over her as he held her tightly.

She'd never liked men to touch her like this. It felt possessive... It was possessive, at least when her father did it to her mother.

But Alessio's grip, his hand placement, felt more like protection, security in the storm. It was peaceful.

Protection? Security?

Brie didn't need protection or security. She took care of herself. She'd learned quickly that the world didn't care for rich kids. Even if they'd been cast out. She'd been on her own for years.

It was difficult, but she'd found her way. She'd graduated, opened a marketing company, found her own footing. She was an independent woman.

Still, Alessio's touch felt nice. Too nice. It reminded her of his fingers on her cheek and the gentle touch of his thumb on her wrist.

She should reclaim her space, but she couldn't make herself do it. In fact, she had to fight the urge to lean her head against his shoulder as the barrage of questions started. That would be too much. It would look overdone, even if it was a natural action.

"Are you excited?"

No. She knew her smile wasn't enough to respond to the reporter's question.

"Any thought to the royal patronages you'll support?" Another question popped off before she could answer the last.

Thank goodness.

"Not yet." She'd never considered the fact that

Alessio might call her name. She'd refused to think of the possibility she might be a princess. The odds were not in her favor…and that was the way she'd wanted it.

"Do you think your family position played any role in your selection?" The reporter's smile wasn't quite a smirk, but she felt Alessio's hand tighten on her waist.

"It was a fair drawing. Are you suggesting otherwise?" Alessio's voice was casual, but she heard the bite behind it.

Which was good, because she knew the answer to that question was that if her family had had their wish, she'd have married at nineteen. It was a choice they'd not even bothered to run past her before making.

"Will your wedding dress be by Ophelia or a royal designer?"

Finally, a reporter's question she could answer… sort of.

"I'm positive that I will wear one of Ophelia's dresses when I marry."

Alessio's fingers tightened on her waist. It wasn't a lie. If she ever married, and Brie was far from sold on the institution, she'd wear one of Ophelia's designs. However, Ophelia's designs would not grace the royal chapel.

At least not on Brie.

A twinge of sadness pressed into her chest. Ophelia's work deserved to be in the royal wedding. If Breanna or her twin sister had won the prize, Ophelia would at least be in the running to design the gown of the decade.

But when Brie didn't wed Prince Alessio, when the ruse was over… She doubted the next royal bride would choose the best friend of the woman who refused to play the part of the lotto bride.

The idea of another woman meeting Alessio at the altar sent a mixture of emotions through her soul. She couldn't quite determine the mixture. It should be relief…should be acceptance. Those were present, but the sadness lingering in the recesses of her body shocked her. Alessio deserved more than a royal union focused on what it brought Celiana.

Would they let him marry for love? Probably not. But at least it wouldn't be the spectacle of a lottery bride. That would be some consolation, right?

"Prince Alessio, do you think your father would be happy with your lotto bride?"

He shifted. Not much. Not enough that she thought anyone in the room noticed. If his arm wasn't around her waist, she wasn't sure she'd have noticed, either.

"I'm sure King Cedric would have been pleased."

They were words. That was the best she could say. It was his interview tone, the one she'd heard so often over the last year. But there was a hint of uncertainty, too. Maybe it was the camera flashes or the casual mention of the man Alessio had called King rather than Father.

Brie slipped her arm around his waist. He was providing her comfort in this sea of uncertainty; she could do the same. And it would look good for the cameras.

His eyes locked with hers and she smiled.

"We forgot to examine you for dirt," he said.

The words were quiet, but she saw a flash of the playful Alessio. That was the magic they needed to tap into.

"If that is the story of the day, remind me to say I told you so." He winked.

If that was the story of the day, the first episode in this marketing adventure was a loss. But he was smiling, and she was looser, too. So she winked back.

"Fair."

For a moment, it was easy to pretend they were a genuine couple. A few minutes of comradery in the storm of whatever this fever dream was.

"How about a kiss for the camera? A proper kiss?"

Her mouth fell open before she clasped it tight and forced a smile back on her face. Kiss. Of course the cameras wanted a kiss. This was a spectacle, after all.

And what was a romantic spectacle without a kiss?

Her fingers shook as she tried to prepare. The idea of kissing Alessio didn't bother her. If he'd dropped his lips to hers a few minutes ago, she might even have swooned a bit. The man was handsome, funny and more relaxed behind closed doors.

She wanted to know how the man beside her, who'd wiped a tear from her cheek, who'd joked about dust and looked like he might like to run away from all this, kissed.

That curiosity was something she'd need to deal with later, without an audience.

But kissing Alessio for the camera, letting the world see her first kiss, felt wrong. A first kiss held power. It contained so much possibility.

Except there wasn't any possibility in their situation.

"I think my future bride has had enough excitement for the day." Alessio's formal tone hung in the room.

What if he doesn't want to kiss me?

Why was that thought banging in her head? This was a charade. A charade. She needed to remember that.

"Are you saying that kissing her Prince Charming would be too exciting?" Lev, a royal commentator who spent most of his time finding fault, however minor, with the royal family, raised a brow.

Prince Charming.

How did the title sound so different when it fell from Lev's mouth?

Lev had spent the last year calling the bride lottery a stunt. He was even hosting an informal betting pool on his website for people to wager how long the royal engagement lasted. The largest bet was placed for three months from today.

The fact that Lev was here was a signal. The royal family wanted to smother his suggestions. Rather than exclude him, they'd made a point of inviting him. If she'd marketed this union, she'd have made the same suggestion.

Media was a game and it was one she was quite skilled at, one that was going to grant her freedom from this trap.

Still, she hated that when she won, it would prove the man right.

"I am quite the kisser. My bride-to-be will certainly swoon the first time our lips connect." The words were said with an over-the-top flair.

Anticipation coated her skin, but she could play into the moment, too. "So sure of yourself."

The audience chuckled, smiles draping everywhere as they clapped for the couple. Good, they were back in control of the narrative. Those that controlled the media narrative won.

Only Lev frowned as he typed something into his phone.

This wasn't real. She knew that, but she hated the look on the gossip reporter's face. She hated that, even unintentionally, they were playing into his expectations.

Brie lifted on her toes, pressing her lips to

Alessio's cheek. The connection was brief, over before she could really think it through.

More than a few calls echoed throughout the crowd for her to do it again, but it was Alessio's reaction that fascinated her.

His jade eyes held hers. The questions and camera flashes evaporated. For a moment, they were the only two people in the crowded room.

"Alessio." His name escaped before she leaned her head against his shoulder.

The day was too much, just as he'd said. The questions, the spotlight, the way the life she'd known had shifted in the space of seconds when Alessio pulled her name.

She was reacting to the day, to the hope of a way out...not to him.

"Shall we get a drink?"

"Please."

Alessio held up a hand. "Briella and I are going to seek refreshments. Enjoy the party. There will be plenty of time for questions during our courtship."

Alessio didn't release her as they walked away from the journalists. His arm was light on her waist. It was a reminder of the role they were playing, and that if she stepped away, everyone would comment.

First lesson—things that seemed meaningless mattered.

She took a deep breath, all hopes of calming herself evaporating as Alessio's scent invaded her senses again. The man was gorgeous, a literal prince… Did he have to smell like heaven, too?

Brie had never allowed herself to fall in lust—not that there'd been many options. Just because she was horrified that her name came out of the giant glass tumbling ball didn't mean she couldn't acknowledge the man beside her was hot.

Right?

Alessio was tall, attractive, kind. There were worse men to play pretend with. Her mouth was dry as she looked at him. His jade gaze met hers and her belly flipped. The man was the definition of *gorgeous*.

A table layered with treats came into view. The decadence reminded her that she was in the palace, next to Alessio as his bride-to-be. She shouldn't need the reminder. She needed to focus, start thinking of her plans and their next steps.

She'd spent her youth looking attentive at boring family functions while drifting away to her own mental space. Even in this ruckus, she should be able to do it. But as his fingers stroked her side, it was impossible to focus on more than his touch.

"This is lovely."

Hints of sugar, lemon and a host of other flavors skipped through her senses. So many sweets finally overtook the delicious scent that was Alessio.

Pastries overloaded the table. Rather than hiring one caterer, Alessio had asked each bakery to deliver a few dozen of their best desserts. That way, everyone got to claim a piece of the day. It was a marketing coup.

"It is." He smiled and looked at the table. "What kind of dessert do you like best?"

"I don't know." She laughed as she looked at the sweets, hoping to cover her uncertainty as she stared at the table. She'd not run in aristocratic circles in years, but she knew the game. Smile, look attentive, even when you feel like falling apart. Muscle memory had been reinforced by years of Ailiono training.

Her mother had not permitted Brie to have sweets as a child or teen. Her family raised her to be…to be exactly where she was, actually. However, her parents would never have attempted to marry her to one of Celiana's princes. Alessio and Sebastian had crowns, but the man her family had wanted her to wed had power. He was a business partner of her father's, a scion of industry with no regard for the women who stood by his side.

Her father's arrangement was for Brie to be his third wife. His third wife and nearly thirty years his junior, she would be the definition of a trophy bride—a young woman he could mold into his "perfect" wife. Only, she wouldn't gain her freedom like the other two had.

Rationally, she knew her mother no longer controlled the food she ate. That just like the outfits she wore, Brie could now choose her food. She was allowed to make her own choices.

She'd not graced her parents' impressive doorstep in almost seven years, but this action… She'd tried so many things since being disowned, but never sweets. Each time she looked at one, considered it, she'd heard her mother's screaming voice, and the urge to taste something had died away.

She didn't have to stay in this restrictive world. Brie had a path out. She could do this.

"I prefer lemon and lavender treats," Alessio said as he handed her a plate, then started putting things on his while making small talk with the person in line before them.

The plate was tiny, embossed with the royal crest at the top and the bottom. Brie knew it only weighed a few ounces, but it was lead in her hand.

She'd overcome so much. This shouldn't be that hard. But still her finger gripped the plate like it might fly from her hands. Her ears buzzed, and she knew people were watching. The longer she stood here, the more likely someone would make this a moment out of their control.

Alessio put a chocolate petit four, a lemon bar and a lavender cookie on his plate, then turned. His eyebrows pulled together as his gaze fell to her empty plate.

"Brie?"

"I don't know what dessert I like." It was such an inconsequential thing, something that wouldn't bother her if she wasn't surrounded by dozens of cameras, in the palace, suddenly engaged to a prince.

She might even make a joke about being a twenty-six-year-old sweet virgin. And she would laugh to cover the past and how it made her different from her peers. She would joke so she didn't have to remember that her family only wanted her if she played by their rigged rules.

"These are my favorite. Try one." He put the cookie on her plate, his fingers tracing along her wrist.

Her breath caught on the connection. Heat raced up her arm as his touch grounded her. She wasn't alone.

"And I do not know what this is, but it's lovely." He set another treat on her plate, leaning forward and pushing a piece of hair behind her ears.

He leaned close, ocean breeze coming with him. Her nerves were still racing, but now they focused on the handsome man's lips brushing her ear.

"You don't have to eat them. Or you can."

She knew the touches, the small talk, even the refreshment table, were designed for the day. It was all a perfect marketing tool for the country and the royal family. If she'd overseen the event, there were a few changes she'd have made, but whoever had planned the occasion was an artist.

And yet, part of her wanted to believe he was caring for her, that the concern sweeping his features was meant only for her. Truly for her. She wanted to believe that if the participants all fell away, if the fancy dresses disappeared and he was in lounge pants and she was in comfy pants no one should see, he'd still care.

Brie smiled. "Thank you. You don't have to hold my hand through all this."

But it's nice.

"You are my bride-to-be." He leaned a little closer. "And the cameras are watching."

Cameras.

The cameras would be focused on the caring prince performing actions for others…not for her.

The press corps surrounding Brie's apartment didn't surprise Alessio. The swarm must have descended as soon as he announced her name. He knew the families with fifty-two entries for their daughters had scheduled security for today, anticipating such an occurrence.

Actually, all the families that could afford the high cost of a year's worth of entries had security. Brie's neighbors were undoubtedly unhappy… and worried.

They needed to fix this. Maybe she could spin this into a "move into the palace with me" post. Yet the public didn't have access to the royal quarters, so there wasn't much of a tourism trap there.

"What the hell!" Brie leaned against him as camera flashes assaulted the tinted windows.

"You won the Princess Lottery." Had she really not expected people to be here?

Brie somehow got closer to him. Her body was warm against his. Maybe it was silly to be so happy with the simple action. But she felt nice against him. They were partners in their goal, two souls from powerful families that craved freedom.

And if it didn't work…if they had to wed to protect Celiana…they'd find a way to make do. Maybe his parents hadn't loved each other, but respect was more than many got.

If there was another way to aid the generations of bakers, shop owners, bistro and hotel operators who based their businesses around honeymooners, reaching for it wasn't selfish. Right?

Alessio had been the rebel. He'd been the runaway unhappy with his role as second fiddle. Stepping in as the dutiful one felt weird, and he wasn't quite sure he was doing it right.

"This is…this is…"

He understood her being at a loss for words. Alessio had grown up in this life, and it was still a game he felt like he was failing at most days.

"It's royal life. The start of it at least. And the role you agreed to play."

Brie's blue eyes flashed. She was gorgeous, and the day was long. The blend of emotions sent desire through his soul. And he ached to protect someone from the world that had finally beaten him.

After all, she hadn't chosen this. Not really. She'd submitted one entry, one tiny slip in a sea of hopefuls, one chance for the crown that would sit on her head forever.

"Only until I get a plan in place that brings more than honeymooners." Brie sighed as the driver pulled as close to her place as the crowd allowed.

"If you can make that happen, then yes. It's temporary. But it might be a good idea to at least consider that it's forever." He paused before adding, "Trust me. If it doesn't work and we meet at the altar, you'll feel better having at least considered it."

If he'd made himself believe his little glass shop was temporary, maybe closing it wouldn't have broken him as much.

"I refuse to think of that until it's absolutely necessary" She pushed away from him, her top teeth digging into her lip.

"Fine. But for now, you're a princess-in-waiting. And the world needs to believe that you believe that." The flash of anger turned to frustration as her bright eyes found his.

"Right. Control the narrative." Brie pulled the bottom of her dress to the side, readying herself to step out.

His life was a series of narratives. Some of them were so well spun, even Alessio wondered what was real and what was the official palace line. It shouldn't bother him that she was speaking in the same tone, but frustration pooled in his soul.

"It's not just about narratives. It's about the country and duty and making sure everyone is safe, even if it means giving up something of yourself."

It was like his father's ghost had spit the words out. They were words the old Alessio would never have spoken.

"Soon you'll have a plan for this country that will bring it more than just honeymooners. And I'll be a blip in the royal family's memory."

Not in my memory.

No matter how long he lived, he wouldn't forget the woman who had marched in after being offered a crown and made a deal to get out of it. How often had he craved the same thing? If her plan worked, he might get back the life he'd had. The life he craved.

Most people only saw the glamour of the crown, not the pain behind it. And now he had the beauty beside him.

"So, what are we going to do?" Fine lines appeared around her eyes. Her lips tipped down before she plastered on a smile. "Move me into the palace?"

He hadn't expected her to suggest it, but he was glad she had, so he didn't have to.

"Yes. You move into the palace. You can make a video telling everyone."

"I was kidding, Your Royal Highness."

Your Royal Highness.

Her back was straight, and she was ready for battle. That was good. Celiana needed strong female role models. And even if they didn't meet at the altar, she'd impress people.

"Brie—" Alessio gestured to the crowd "—you won the Princess Lottery."

"We have a deal, Your Royal Highness."

"Do you plan to call me Your Royal Highness whenever you're frustrated? Not that I'm complaining… Well, not really. It will make it easy to determine when you are cross." He tapped his head. "Mental note made."

"This isn't a joke."

He agreed, but humor helped in difficult moments. It relaxed people. He'd been good at it once upon a time. That man seemed to want to emerge around Brie. He'd have to wrestle him back into the mental cage he thought he'd thrown away the key to.

The crowd was getting impatient.

"You can't stay here. It's not safe." He gestured to the sea of people.

Most of them just wanted a picture of the royal couple. They wanted to tell their friends and future grandkids where they'd been when Prince Alessio and Princess Briella arrived at her home.

But there were others. People who despised the monarchy and people who blamed the hard years on the royals.

It wasn't fair. Celiana was a constitutional monarchy. King Sebastian was little more than a figurehead. But the royals were the faces of the country. They were the attraction that drove tourism. Real-life fairy-tale creatures, they played a role with perceived, if little actual, power.

And the last few years had been hard. The economic downturn had hit nearly every sector and there were more than a few disgruntled citizens. And even if there weren't, that didn't mean that a future royal bride should live unprotected. Even one who never planned to wear the crown.

She sighed but didn't wilt. Her eyes roamed the crowd, and he saw acceptance register.

It was good, but it tore at him, too. Acceptance was part of the royal life. He and Sebastian had learned at an early age that their wills, their desires, all came at least second to the needs of the country. It was a lesson Brie would face again and again, too. Particularly if they wed.

His choices had evaporated the moment his father had his stroke. But hers... Until today they'd been wide open. The ease of life, the ability to just run to the store or go to work...all were gone for her, at least for a while.

"You're right. I can't stay here."

Brie's words pulled him away from his unsettled thoughts. He had to focus on the present. The past was lost, and the future was a reminder that his life was scripted now. *Focus on the here and now.*

"We'll pack up some of your stuff now, then I can send the staff to get the rest."

"Sure." Brie nodded. He could see that a fight was brewing in her eyes, but she was ceding the ground on this. A battle won.

"Princess! Princess!" The calls echoed as security opened the car door.

Brie raised a hand, smiling as she moved through

the crowd, ignoring the questions and moving as quickly as security created the path for them.

She shut her apartment door behind them and crossed her arms. "This is too much."

"This is what winning the lottery looks like." The rules were clear. Each entry was a contract. By putting your name in the crystal ball you agreed that, if chosen, you became a princess.

"I'm aware of that, Alessio."

"She entered *for* me." A woman stepped from what had to be Brie's bedroom. "I am so sorry."

"Ophelia." Brie ran to her friend.

She held on tightly, and Alessio was grateful she had someone to pour herself into. And he was jealous there wasn't anyone who'd do the same for him. He glanced around the apartment, looking for a way to give them privacy, but it was too tiny.

"I shouldn't have agreed to the marketing strategy. This is a nightmare." Ophelia's voice shook as she looked to Alessio.

Before he could say anything, Brie squeezed her friend, then stepped back. "Not ideal, but at least this fiancé is cuter than the one my parents lined up."

"Closer to your age, too." Ophelia's laughter mingled with Brie's. "But this isn't the time for jokes."

She'd been engaged? That didn't make sense. The Ailionos made huge engagement announcements. Her parents' engagement party had cost more than his parents' wedding.

And she wasn't in contact with her family. Her

family had disowned her...at least according to the not-so-quiet rumors.

Engaged.

The word tapped against his brain.

His life was a series of long days, but he was officially overloaded.

"Engaged?"

"Not important."

He wasn't aware he'd spoken until Brie waved it away. But he saw her shoulders tighten—so it wasn't unimportant. Another question for another day, then.

If there was a spurned ex waiting, well, he at least needed to make sure security knew. That was the reason for his curiosity. The only reason...

He almost believed that.

"I came to see if you wanted me to spirit you off the island. Not sure how, but Rafael and I planned to work that out later. Bringing *him* makes that harder."

Ophelia tilted her head as she looked at Alessio, sizing him up. He didn't shift under her judgment, but that didn't mean he didn't want to.

"Not impossible. Just harder." Ophelia raised a brow.

"No escape needed." Brie shook her head and moved to his side. She was close to him but careful not to touch him. There were no cameras here, no reason to pretend they were starting the journey of falling in love.

"I have a plan." Brie nodded to the door where

the crowd was audible. "And my plans always work out."

Ophelia opened her mouth but said nothing.

But he could hear the concern. No one got everything. But this…this he wanted Brie to achieve. For her peace…and his.

"I'll get the dress back to you tomorrow, if that works?"

Her friend crossed her arms. "I assume the palace will purchase it. They often put high-profile outfits in the fashion museum." Ophelia's eyes held his, daring him to contradict her. "I think this one counts."

"Ophelia—"

"Send the bill." Alessio looked at Brie. "After all, it would be expected."

"Of course." There was a look in her eyes. Did she wish he'd said something else?

No. They were just tired.

"I will send the bill first thing in the morning, Your Royal Highness." Ophelia stepped to them and pulled Brie into her arms.

"I meant what I said," she said to Brie. "Say the word and I will find a way to get you out of this." She kissed her cheek, then stepped back.

"Thank you." Brie took a deep breath. "Alessio, while I gather a few things, can you make sure security helps Ophelia get to her vehicle without being accosted by the crowd?"

"Of course."

Brie moved to her room.

Before he could open the door, Ophelia put her hand on his chest. "She's had a lifetime of hurt. You do not get to add to it. So, if you hurt her, crown or not, you *will* answer to me."

The threat wasn't needed, but he was glad Brie had someone in her corner.

"Understood."

"Good." Ophelia nodded then listened as he gave the security team directions for her safety.

As soon as Ophelia was out the door, he heard Brie shout from the other room.

"Alessio!"

He moved as quickly as his feet would carry him. Had someone broken in? Sebastian had once had a girlfriend who was stalked by individuals hoping to capture a picture to sell to the press. A few had even broken into her place, foolish hope of quick money outweighing rational thoughts of jail time.

Brie's apartment would be easy to get into, and the lotto bride picture would be worth thousands!

The small apartment was sparsely furnished. The only photos appeared to be of her, Ophelia and a man he guessed was Ophelia's husband. The apartment was close to public transportation, and was the kind of place university students and those just starting in their careers chose.

It was not a place one expected to find an Ailiono. Her room at the Ailiono mansion was likely larger than this space. What was she doing here?

"I made a mistake letting Ophelia leave." Brie's

hands were on her chest, and her eyes were tired. The weight of everything seemed to press against her.

"Oh." Alessio wasn't sure what to say. "I thought you weren't escaping."

If she left immediately, would they ask him to draw another name? How selfish was he for considering that? When they broke up in a few weeks, he could pretend to be heartbroken. But today...

"I told you I could prove this stunt unnecessary."

"You did, but it's a lot. You know it and I know it." Alessio knew his voice was too tight, but while he wanted to believe in the possibility, reality was difficult to avoid for a royal.

"I meant that. I'm not running." The last sentence was tight, and he could see her shift slightly.

Not yet.

He'd run. He knew the look. But she was here now.

"Brie—"

"It's the dress," she interrupted, gesturing to herself. "The dress," she repeated as her eyes fell to the floor.

He wasn't sure what the issue was.

"It is gorgeous."

He marveled at the deep green, and the low neckline with a simple necklace. She was beautiful, but the dress turned her into a nymph, a mythical creature almost too beautiful to touch.

"Yes, it's beautiful. Some of Ophelia's best work, but I'm buttoned into it."

She turned, and he saw tiny buttons starting at the base of her neck, all the way to the top of her incredible butt.

He swallowed the burst of need pushing at him.

She looked over her shoulder, pulling her braid to the side. "Can you, please?"

"Of…course."

Stepping up, he lifted his hands and started undoing the delicate pearl buttons. Her skin appeared by centimeters. A tiny mole on her shoulder, a freckle in the middle of her back. He'd never been turned on by so little, but Alessio ached to run his finger along the edges of skin he was revealing.

He would not betray this moment. She'd asked him for aid so he would ignore the fact that he wanted to trail kisses across her back, wanted to strip the dress down. He cleared his throat as he refocused on the buttons. The rebel prince pushing against the dutiful man he needed to be.

"You all right?"

No.

"Fine." He breathed the word into being. He made it to the middle of her back and let out a sigh of relief.

"Is something on my back?"

"No." The word did nothing to stop the pulsating bead of need in his soul. It didn't clear the thoughts or the desire; if anything, the fuse seemed to speed up.

"You're perfection." Alessio's finger slipped, connecting with her bare skin. Desire blazed through him. What would she do if he kissed her? What would she taste like?

Fire? Passion?

"Think you can take it from here?" Alessio barely got the words out.

"No." Brie looked over her shoulder. "I mean... it's just, the pearls are sewn on by hand. It's so delicate. I can't see the buttons. I wore it to highlight her ability, given that you required a wedding dress."

"Actually, that was Sebastian." Alessio let out a sigh. This was a topic he could use to alleviate some of the need clawing through him.

Brie spun. Her hands clasped the top of the dress to keep it in place.

All hope of ignoring the desire evaporated. Her chest was pink...with frustration...or might she be pulsing with need, too?

His body ached as he made sure to keep his gaze focused on her face, when all he wanted to do was worship her with his lips. His tongue...

"Your brother?"

Focus, Alessio. Focus.

"He's still learning his words carry more weight. The Princess Lottery was my father's idea, the reason I came back." That was close to the truth.

"You came back for this. I might have stayed—" Her blue eyes caught his. "Where were you?"

"Not in Celiana." He didn't discuss those years. The happiness, the freedom...

"Right." He started to push his hands into his

pockets before adjusting his stance. "Sebastian... Well, he thought the idea wild and hasn't kept his thoughts quiet."

"He's different." Brie looked at Alessio.

"The crown is heavy." That was another topic he wasn't going to discuss. Sebastian wasn't the same. He skipped duties. He seemed uninterested in the role he'd practiced for since birth.

"Good thing we aren't getting married... We might have to answer each other's questions." Brie pursed her lips.

Not necessarily.

That was a sad truth of royal life. As long as you looked happy to the outside, you could do almost anything behind the walls of the palace.

"Sebastian joked that I should have everyone arrive in wedding dresses, and before I knew what happened, they wrote it into the contract. Luckily, most people rented their gowns."

"Rented?" Brie's mouth fell open.

"Yes." He made a twirling motion with his finger, and she turned as he restarted his undressing mission. "I worked out a deal with one of the chain bridal gown places in America. The women could rent their gowns, then ship them back. If one of the women with a rented gown won, the chain would get to dress the princess on our wedding day."

"That was very kind." She bent her head, and his fingers slipped again.

The contact between his fingers and her bare

skin lasted less than a second. It was no time at all and forever all at once.

"I think…" she started, but didn't continue for a moment. "I think I've got it from here."

"Of course." His feet screamed as he stepped away. "I'll…" Words were difficult to muster. "Should I pack anything in the living room or kitchen?"

"No."

He headed for the door.

"Alessio?" Her cheeks were pink; her lips pursed. Brie's hands clutched the bodice of her gown. She started toward him, then stopped.

"Yes?"

"Thank you." Her smile was soft. It wasn't a brilliant, excited grin or joyous beam, but it filled her eyes. "Today was a long day."

"Tomorrow is the start of the next chapter." Whether that ended in their freedom or at the altar was still too early for Alessio to know.

"I look forward to showing you how we save Celiana without sacrificing our own happiness."

"I hope you do." He stepped out of her room to give her space. Privacy was something in short supply within the palace walls where she'd be living—at least for a few weeks.

And maybe forever.

CHAPTER THREE

ALESSIO STOOD IN front of Briella's door. He needed to knock. It was nearly nine in the morning; time was moving fast. His bride-to-be was a stranger. They didn't need to know each other's secrets, but they needed to know enough to put on a good show.

That was all people really wanted. It was a sad truth he'd learned as soon as he was old enough to understand the news articles printed about his family. A smiling family was best. The press could translate any frown into a generational fight in an instant. Truth was only good if the gossip was boring.

And the gossip was never boring.

Brie was part of this now whether or not she wanted it—at least for a while.

The hint of his old self was rooting for Brie.

But the man standing in front of her door this morning was Prince Alessio, heir to the kingdom and man at the center of the Princess Lottery scheme.

The scheme could very well result in Briella Ailiono meeting him at the altar. The further he got away from her enthusiasm, the more he figured that would be the outcome. Maybe she was a marketing genius—he wanted to hope so because no matter how much he'd run through the deal last night, Alessio had found no ideas to help her.

Celiana was a kingdom built on honeymoon tourists. When they'd vanished, so had much of the prosperity. The tourism board had run a few ad campaigns, but none of them had resulted in much. The honeymooners had stayed away...until the Princess Lottery.

The morning was already slipping away, and he'd yet to greet her, yet to see the woman who might very well be his wife. In the palace, everything was scheduled. And on the schedule for the day was "Get to know the lotto bride."

His secretary had actually written those words. *Lotto bride.* It was a descriptor that would follow Brie for the rest of her days.

Unless she pulled off the unthinkable. Then she'd get her freedom...and so would he. Maybe he could go back to Scotland. He'd sold his shop, but he'd opened one once before and he could do it again. Except living incognito after being the international face of the Princess Lottery wouldn't work.

It had barely worked the first time. Every once in a while, people would recognize him, but he'd been able to play off the doppelgänger idea. After all, no one expected a prince in a glass shop.

It could work again—but he'd have to have security. It was something he probably should have had before. But his father had refused to provide it since he'd "walked out on duty."

Alessio squeezed his eyes closed. No. He couldn't

give in to that fancy. Even if she had figured out a brilliant plan, there was no guarantee. He'd tasted freedom once. Giving it up had destroyed a sizable portion of his soul.

Brie could hope. Alessio couldn't afford it.

Today was about preparation, informing her what she should expect.

Everyone would snap pictures of her.

Language lacked descriptors for Brie's beauty. She was ethereal. Unbuttoning her gown last night was nearly a spiritual experience.

His subconscious had spun that moment into heated dreams. He was attracted to her. How could he not be? But it was her strength that echoed through his heart. How many women would challenge a prince the moment they met him?

He needed to knock, start the day's agenda by going over the rules, the expectations. He had to explain the bars of the gilded cage that was hers now.

How was he supposed to do that?

"You look weird hovering in front of her door, brother." Sebastian's tone was relaxed. Jokey... unbothered.

Unbothered.

That was once the descriptor applied by his father to Alessio. Sebastian was dutiful. The obedient son. The one who did what was expected... until his father passed.

Now the man was unbothered by everything.

Despite the crown on his head. It was infuriating. But given that the last argument Alessio had had with the king of Celiana resulted in his brother's coronation, Alessio had sworn not to argue.

Bury the emotions. Deal with it privately.

"Good observation, Sebastian." Alessio turned, wondering what would happen if Brie opened the door to find the king and her fiancé facing off.

"Aren't your rooms connected?" Sebastian leaned against the wall.

"Yes." His brother knew that; he was just pointing out that Alessio didn't have to be out here. But he did. He was trying to make Brie feel less trapped.

"Trying to work up courage?"

He wanted to deny it, but what was the point? He'd been caught. And he needed courage. Though that wasn't all he needed.

Part of him, the rebel prince who cried out in her presence, wanted to open the door, pull Brie into his arms and see if the heat burning between them last night was still there.

"Did you need something?"

"I'd like to remind you that no one forced you to follow through with the king's plan." Sebastian looked at his fingers then back at Alessio.

The king's plan.

"You're the king and you didn't have any better ideas." Alessio didn't like the hint of bitterness in his tone.

The royal family's only actual power was influence, but it was influence his brother seemed inclined to ignore for as long as possible. Their father was gone; if they didn't step up, who would?

"Maybe you should have worn the crown."

Alessio laughed. "King Cedric is rolling in his fancy tomb hearing that."

His father had spent his life pointing out Alessio's flaws. Getting away had been so healing. It was ironic that he'd finally become the prince his father wanted.

If King Cedric was here, I'd still be free.

"You wear the crown well." It wasn't the truth, but maybe one day it would be.

"We both know that's a lie." Sebastian knocked on Brie's door.

"Wai—" Alessio's mouth froze as his brother rapped his knuckles again.

They waited a moment, but Brie didn't answer. His stomach hit the floor. Surely, she hadn't fled…

"Rattling you is fun. Hard since you came back. But fun." His brother winked. "Your bride-to-be was in the kitchen at four thirty. She's now installed in the media room in the east wing."

"We only have one media room," Alessio grumbled as he started toward where his fiancée was hiding.

Four thirty.

He was an early riser by necessity. If he wanted any time to himself, he took it before the world woke. He'd go for a run or a swim a little after five thirty and have breakfast by six fifteen.

However, when he owned his life, Alessio regularly waited until eight or nine to begin his day.

Stop thinking of that.

It was the past. Focus on Brie. On the here and now.

"She's under your skin."

"She's…"

Alessio pushed his hands into his pockets then pulled them out as words refused to come to mind. Brie wasn't under his skin; it was the thought that her idea, her plan, whatever she'd figured out, might actually work. There was the rush freedom brought, the hint that maybe the life he'd had could be his again.

Still, he did not get ruffled, not anymore. That was Sebastian's role.

Alessio was cool, calm and dutiful. The prince everyone expected…the one the island needed.

"There is one thing we should discuss before you greet Briella *Ailiono*."

The inflection on her last name gave away the issue. "Her family."

"So you've thought of it, too?"

Not really. Not in the way that seemed to echo off his brother. He'd seen her panic yesterday at the dessert table. Heard the jokes that cut too close to her soul about an engagement to a man evidently many years her senior.

Her family had let Brie down. He understood that. She'd flown from her cage and landed in another. Just like him.

"She's estranged. The entire court knows that." The reasons for it were for Brie to acknowledge, not him.

Her panic at the dessert table yesterday had made Alessio see red. That she'd panic at such a thing implied the control she'd endured growing up.

Luckily, he'd kept his cool for the cameras.

"Do you know why she's estranged?"

"No. But it hardly matters. If the Ailiono family has issues with this union, they will go through me."

Brie was smart and kind—the woman had entered the bridal lottery solely to help her friend, and had protected Ophelia last night, too. Maybe those weren't qualities the Ailiono family valued, but they were ones he did.

Sebastian's head snapped back. "Going toe-to-toe with the Ailionos might not work. They have more power."

"More land, more money...power—they probably think so. But no one has ever really tested that." Alessio didn't wish to break that ground, but if Brie needed it... Well, the royal family would offer her protection. There had to be some bonus to wearing a crown.

"You'd challenge the Ailiono clan?"

"If necessary." Maybe it was weird to feel so protective of Briella. But it was the least he could do. She was under his protection for as long as she was his fiancée…and for forever if they met at the altar.

"You don't have to marry her."

"Good. Something we agree on." Brie was smiling as she held the door open.

For once Alessio wished the palace staff didn't keep the door hinges so well oiled.

"Brie. You look lovely this morning."

Alessio dipped his head, unable to keep the smile from his lips. She was gorgeous and so sure of herself. Once more his heart swelled with the idea of freedom. Of escaping…with Brie.

Except that if they escaped, it wouldn't be together. His happiness deflated a little on that realization.

"I've breakfast in here for you, Alessio. There is enough, if you'd like to come to the presentation, too, Your Majesty."

"Sebastian." The king tilted his head. "You are to be my sister-in-law after all."

"We'll see about that."

"I *like* her." Sebastian nodded to Brie, then turned to Alessio. His brother didn't hide his chuckle as he walked away. It was still weird to hear Sebastian laugh.

"A presentation?" Alessio stepped into the media room and felt his mouth fall open.

One side of the room looked like a miniature studio with a ring light, green screen and laptop set up. The other side indicated she'd found the library and carted what looked like dozens of books.

How long had she been awake?

"Did you get any sleep, Brie?"

"I did." She smiled, hesitating before adding, "Thank you for asking."

The hesitation before her thanks nearly broke his heart. It was a simple question. A kind one. And he could tell that no one usually asked.

No one asked him, either. How he wished they shared more in common than family trauma.

"How?" He blew out a breath as he surveyed the media room.

"I slept here." Brie grinned. "The couch is surprisingly comfortable."

Alessio shook his head. "I haven't slept on a couch since I was a teen trying to make King Cedric mad."

He couldn't even remember the argument now. There'd been so many with his father. But the result was Alessio sleeping on the same couch Brie had for almost a month until he had finally relented on whatever the fight was about. Which was why he didn't remember the reason. He only remembered the fight his father had won.

Though since he was back in Celiana, his father had won that one, too. Not that he'd ever known it.

"Why do you call him King Cedric?"

Alessio took the coffee from Brie's hand, her fingers brushing his. The lightening he'd experienced at her touch last night reappeared immediately.

He took a long sip, before asking, "What else would I call him?"

Brie's eyes widened.

"I fear I said a princely thing."

"A princely thing?" Brie moved to the small table where fruits, scones and breakfast meats were laid out. "What does that mean?"

Alessio made up his own plate then followed her to the couch. "Oh. It's a thing that makes people realize Sebastian and I aren't normal. That our upbringing was…unique."

Unique was as good a word as any.

"I called him King Cedric because that was his title."

In his mind it made sense. He knew others viewed their parents differently. He cared for his mother, loved her. His father, on the other hand… He'd respected his devotion to Celiana. If a little of it was ever directed toward him— Alessio shut the thought down.

His father had done the best he could for the country, but he'd seen Alessio and Sebastian as extensions of his duty more than as sons.

"Alessio…"

Brie's eyes held a look he knew was pity. He didn't need it. Didn't want it—particularly from her.

"Presentation time." Alessio clapped his hands. "We have a wedding to stop!"

A wedding to stop.

Those were words Brie desperately wanted to hear, so why did they turn her skin cold?

Alessio, the rebel turned dutiful heir to the throne, was a mystery. He'd spent his teen years avoiding royal duties, arriving almost late to events and ducking out early. It was typical teen behavior—but as a prince the press had labeled him a rebel. And he'd seemed to lean in to the role.

Brie mentally shook herself. This wasn't a mystery she needed to crack. She needed his support, which he seemed willing to give. But he'd dodged every deep question she'd asked.

That didn't matter. It didn't.

A yawn gathered at the back of her throat, and Brie forced it away. There wasn't time for exhaustion. She'd worked through the night. Literally. She'd taken catnaps on the couch, woken and re-started.

Brie had pulled all-nighters at university. Her parents had cut her off just after her first semester, when she'd made it clear she had no intention of marrying her father's business contact. From that moment, the payments for school all fell to her.

But for the first time in her life, she could make her own choices. So she'd taken out a loan and made it her goal to graduate in three years instead of four. Working as a barista on campus, studying on every break and going on less than five hours of sleep most nights nearly broke her.

Her family had hoped she'd break, that she'd come crawling back and do what they wanted. Follow their plans. But doing that meant never getting a say in the choices of her own life.

Was that what had happened to Alessio? Why he was back? He'd spent three years abroad, and the royal family had said nothing of his whereabouts. It was like he'd vanished to another dimension, only to reappear when his father, the man he only called King Cedric, suffered his stroke.

The royal family had welcomed him back. They'd pretended like the years away never occurred. Her family would do the same if she bowed the knee and agreed to marry a business contact or foreign heir, if she added value to the family firm. It wasn't as if the Ailionos needed more.

Part of her did wonder about the conversation, if there was any, around the dinner table last night. Her mother had made her thoughts on the Princess Lottery clear when a reporter asked her about it at a ladies' charity event. It was an event Brie knew her mother didn't want to be at, but appearances were what mattered.

According to her mother, the lottery was gauche and in poor taste for the royal family. She'd said that no one would treat the lotto winner like a real princess and that she thought the whole thing ridiculous. She'd not commented when asked about Brie's participation.

"What was your favorite dress Ophelia made?" His question broke through her tired brain.

"The one I wore yesterday." Brie grinned as she pulled up the presentation slides. "I know white is tradition, for some pretty horrid reasons in my mind. Purity." She made a face. If that was important to a person, then fine, but it wasn't important to her, and that should be fine, too.

"A little old-fashioned, true. The color of a gown should be a bride's choice, for whatever reason she likes. Of course, it needs to be coordinated with the groom."

"So he gets a say?" Brie raised a brow. She had no plans to meet Alessio at the altar, so the argument was pointless, but she couldn't seem to stop herself. "I thought the day was about the bride?"

"But what if she wears orange, and he's in blue? A color clash in their photos! Forever, Brie. Think of the pictures!"

Brie shook her head as the laughter bubbled up. The silly Alessio was here. The one that sat on the floor with her yesterday. The one she needed beside her for this campaign to work.

"That is ridiculous!"

"It is." Alessio leaned toward her, and her eyes fell to his lips. Round, full...so close. "But it made you laugh."

A joke. It was perfect. He'd not questioned her statement on bridal purity. Instead, he'd made a joke about color theory. It was silly and there was no judgment in his voice.

Not that there was much to tell about her love life. Brie had never been with a man, and at twenty-six it made her feel awkward sometimes. But that was better than the alternatives.

She was an Ailiono, which meant everyone who'd asked her out wanted her because of her family. No one wanted her for her, and she wasn't willing to give her heart away for less.

Maybe once she made her own way, found her own path. But deep down she worried she couldn't run far enough to be free of the Ailiono name.

"I love the deep green, the buttons. I obviously can't wear it for my wedding day, though." She saw his lips twitch on the words *wedding day*. The giant white elephant in the room.

"If we marry, you can wear any color on our wedding day. The jade highlights your eyes, gives you a fairylike appearance. And acknowledges your strength, your ability to step away from tradition. But I must know the color so my tie coordinates."

A lump pressed against her throat. What was she to say to that? He'd told her to prepare in case they married, in case she couldn't pull it off. And for just a moment, she let herself visualize marrying Alessio.

He'd be so much better than any man her family would choose. But he wasn't her choice. Not really.

It was just years of loneliness reacting to his silliness and an acknowledgment of a kindred soul. He was a man caught in the same storm of family expectations.

The memory of him unbuttoning her dress flared in her mind. Her body had ached for release. Her brain had screamed for his lips to trail the path of the buttons. Her body had shuddered as his fingers brushed her skin. If he'd asked to kiss her…

She cleared her throat. Time to put away intrusive thoughts about the man before her. The prince. Her fiancé.

Her fake fiancé.

"Let's get the show started."

Alessio turned his focus to the smart board she had hooked up to the laptop. "All right. Show me what you've got."

Brie saw the hint of hope and the moment he cleared it from his face. He wanted to believe this was possible, but he wasn't willing to fully give in to the thought. Would that hurt her plans?

She wasn't sure.

"All right, so you ran the bride lottery to rejuvenate tourism, correct?"

"My father pointed out, just before his stroke—" Alessio paused, made a clicking noise with his tongue, then started again. "We were once the honeymoon capital of the world, Brie. Many of our shops, our bakeries, rely on the tourist traffic."

"You're right," Brie conceded.

It was an issue she'd acknowledged in her research last night. The number of families that relied on revenue from honeymoon tourists was far larger than she'd realized.

And the tourism bounce the Princess Lottery had brought was real. In fact, she'd spent a solid hour last night running numbers and trying to control the panic building in her soul. The country clearly needed the fairy tale.

But that reliance was, also a weakness.

"I might have looked for another option, maybe. But then the Ocean Falls Hotel—"

"Closed last year," she interrupted.

This was her presentation. Focusing on failures was a recipe for disaster. She'd listened to more than one professor drum on the need to focus briefly on the past then force the client to look at the future, at the bright picture you wanted them to see.

She continued, "The upgrades needed to bring the historic building into the twenty-first century were too much for the current owners. I've heard rumors of a corporation stepping in. So it might reopen."

She hoped it did, even if she'd never stayed there. The Ailionos did not stay in regular hotels, and once she'd been cut off, she couldn't afford a night. But she'd listened to tourists in the bistro talk about the murals and salt baths. The closure was a devastating blow to the local economy.

"Your family are buying it?"

Could they still be called her family? She supposed she carried their last name. Their DNA created her. Her mother had spent her entire childhood using knife-edged compliments to sculpt her into the perfect Ailiono bride: submissive, willing to do whatever the family asked.

Her father was never home. His life was spent at the office or with one of his many mistresses. She was only a thing to be bartered for his power.

The only thing her parents had agreed on in the last decade was her dismissal from the family firm.

"I'm not privy to the inner choices of the Ailiono firm, but if I had to guess…yes." She shrugged.

According to reports, the hotel needed extensive renovations. The historical beauty was crumbling from the inside. Her family was one of the few with the resources to accomplish such a task.

"Tourists—"

"Do not need to be honeymooners," Brie interrupted again. "We've limited ourselves by catering only to them. All the efforts the tourism board made were to court honeymooners, not tourists in general. The island revolves around love, but it doesn't need to."

She waited, but he didn't offer anything, so she moved to the next slide. "The Falls of Oneiros, the market stalls stuffed with goods from around the world, the Ruins of Epiales, the hiking trails, the art scene, which is world-class, cuisine that is spectacular—a place foodies should flock to—we have it all here."

Brie sucked in a breath, nerves making her rush. "In short, we've got something for most kinds of tourists, and we're limiting ourselves by focusing our efforts on honeymooners. Marriages fail, even if they don't end in divorce, and return trips are few and far between."

"Such a dismal statement." Alessio crossed his arms.

"I know King Cedric and Queen Genevieve's union was the stuff of legends."

Alessio made a face but didn't add anything. Her parents' union was the stuff crafted from the worst nightmares.

"Not every marriage is a success story. And there are people who never wish to marry. They have had bad marriages and won't want to travel to an island of love. They are people who could bring their money to this kingdom but won't if we are only a honeymoon destination. That is the mistake we have made so many times. We can be more. The country *needs* to be more."

Alessio's stance loosened as he leaned forward,

his hands resting on his thighs as he looked at her screen. "How?"

The urge to clap nearly consumed her. She knew this moment. She'd seen it in meetings, when a client who'd been uncertain saw her pitch and knew it had possibilities. That was when the momentum shifted her way.

She was going to gain her freedom.

Hidden under the joy was a pinch of something, a pain that shouldn't be there. She didn't want to marry Alessio. She didn't. So why was there anything besides joy?

"We—" she pointed to him, then herself, ignoring the bite of discomfort in her belly "—do all the things." She flipped to the next slide, focusing on the joy winning brought. "We use the bride lottery and our 'impending nuptials'—" she put the words in air quotes "—as the marketing. Everyone will follow us anyway, so we become tourists in our kingdom. While the world looks at us, we market everything Celiana offers. We use my social media platform and engage with people, but talk about everything but the wedding."

"Everything but the wedding?"

"Yes. We'll refer to each other as fiancé and act the part some."

"All part of the show." Alessio nodded.

Show.

It was the right word, but Brie hated it. Still, those were the roles they were playing.

He stood, stepping toward her. Her heart picked up, the annoying organ steadfastly ignoring her brain's commands to stay calm. Alessio smelled divine this morning, the smile on his lips, the twinkle in his green eyes for her...

"This might work." His hand reached for hers, the connection blasting through her.

Her tongue was stuck to the roof of her mouth. Once more her brain issued the orders to say yes. One did not fall in love fast. In lust, however... Well, that box was already checked. But who wouldn't lust after the Adonis standing before her?

"It will work." It didn't sound as confident as she'd like. "And we can start today." She moved to pull up her plans to hike the trail, but Alessio's fingers tightened on her wrist before he let her go.

She looked at him. The prince stood here now. The silly rebel was gone. This was the man she'd seen on television. It was a subtle shift: a tightening in the shoulders, a tip of the lips, a coolness in the eyes. Here stood Alessio the dutiful.

"We are not starting today."

If her breath was thready and uncertain, his was firm. There was no hint that the touch between them was driving lustful thoughts through every inch of his body.

"Alessio," she began, thinking maybe she wasn't the dutiful daughter of the Ailiono family now, but it was the role her family had groomed her for. It was a mask she could slide back on. "This is a good plan."

"It has promise."

Promise!

Before she could argue, he reached for her wrist again. Once more her body betrayed her. Her chest loosened, her skin heated and an ache to lean closer poured through her. There was a pull she'd never felt before, one she needed to ignore, no matter how much her body might yearn to explore it.

"But tomorrow is an early enough start date. You've been up all night." His fingers ran along her palm.

Pulling herself together, she stepped away from his touch. She needed to focus. "I'm used to it."

"Just because you are used to it doesn't mean that you should be." His voice was velvet. A calm water. That was what he felt like.

There was the urge to relax that pulled at her. She'd never given in to that impulse when her life was overwhelming. And if she'd given in, if she'd returned to her family, she'd have lost everything.

Brie couldn't give in now, either.

She raised her chin. "I'm not weak."

That was the word her mother had thrown at her over and over. Eat too much: she was weak. Get anything less than an A-plus on homework: weak. Rebel against family plans: weak.

"I hate that you feel the need to defend rest."

Who was he to say that? Since returning to the

island, Alessio had worked tirelessly. It was all he did.

"How often do you rest? You and your brother have reversed roles. He plays and you—" She cut herself off. This was not an argument they needed to have.

Alessio raised a brow. "Don't hold back. I can take it."

My feelings never matter, so say it.

That was the underlying statement. Why was it so easy to read him?

Because they were two sides of the same coin.

"What does everyone say about me, Brie?"

"That you work yourself to the bone for Celiana. That you've changed. That maybe you should have been king."

Alessio shuddered. "I am not the king. Just a prince serving his country." He closed his eyes for a second, then opened them and offered a smile. "It's a good plan, but starting tomorrow is good enough. Rest today. You will be on the go for as long as you are in the palace."

Maybe forever. He didn't say those words, but she heard them in the quiet.

Fine. She could rest today, but there was still something else, something she'd thought about too much since her name left his lips yesterday.

Her insides quaked. She could do this…she had to.

"There is one other thing." Her voice shook, and his eyes softened.

He read people well. That was good, but it also meant he paid attention, and no one had ever paid attention to her. Not really.

"Brie?"

Say the words, Brie.

Her mind was screaming; blood pounded in her ears.

"We should kiss." She swallowed the lump in her throat before pointing to the ring light. "For the camera."

"For the camera?" Alessio looked at the setup. "Is that necessary?"

"We need to put something out today. Control the narrative. And people wanted to see us kiss yesterday. This will be a good teaser for tomorrow."

"Teaser?" Alessio blew out a breath. Maybe he didn't want to kiss her, but it needed to happen.

"There's more." He raised an eyebrow but didn't interrupt. Which was good, because if she didn't rush this next part, she might not get it out. "I want to kiss before we do it for the camera. I don't want my first kiss to be for an audience...even one we are controlling."

"First kiss?"

There was no way to miss his shock. What was she to say?

The truth.

Brie did her best not to drop his gaze.

"Yes."

The word shook as it exited her mouth, and she

clenched her fingers. This wasn't a big deal... Well, a first kiss might be. She'd hoped it would be—once—but those girlish dreams had died years ago.

At least she thought they had. Last night she'd nearly turned and kissed him. Kissing Alessio didn't frighten her; in fact, she wanted it. More than she'd wanted something in a long time.

And yet he just stood there, his green eyes boring through her.

"My engagement was arranged and not for long." Brie cleared her throat, not wanting to travel that road right now. "And the Ailiono name means the few dates I've been on in the last few years were epic failures."

She didn't owe him an explanation but once she started it the words tumbled forth.

"Relax." Alessio's arm wrapped around her waist, the weight of it heavy against her back. "Breathe."

She took a deep breath, looked at him, and still nothing.

"If you don't want..."

He placed a finger over her lips and dropped his forehead to hers. "I want to kiss you, Brie."

The words were soft, and hard, and her body tightened. Flutters of excitement raced across her skin. His scent wrapped around her.

"But I'm not going to kiss you."

That stung. In the softest, gooiest part of her soul. A place she never let anyone in.

"This moment deserves to be yours. As special as I can make it. So, you're going to kiss me." He opened his eyes, his lips so close. "This moment is yours, Briella. All yours."

She waited only a moment before brushing her lips against his. The touch was so light—so unsatisfying.

Closing the tiny distance between them, she wrapped her arms around his neck. If this was her first kiss, she was making it memorable. Her nerves vanished as she grazed his lips again.

His hand trailed along her back, each flick adding more heat to the internal inferno he'd awoken. His other hand lingered on her cheek, his thumb rubbing against her jaw.

Brie let her body lead as she opened her mouth. His tongue met hers and her world exploded. She pulled him closer, though she wasn't sure how it was physically possible.

He tasted of coffee and scones and life. *Life.* It was a weird description, but it felt so true. She had plans, goals, but much of her life was lived in stasis, waiting to really begin. Here, now, it felt like something so much more.

Finally, she released him. The nerves that had vanished in his arms roared back immediately. What was one to say after they'd kissed a prince?

After acknowledging their lack of experience? When their entire body seemed to sing?

Silence hung between them.

"Maybe we should have videoed that." Brie let out a nervous laugh. In the realm of good things to say after a first kiss that was at the bottom of any list.

She straightened her shoulders and pointed to the media setup. "Round two?"

"This is your show." A look passed over Alessio's features, but whatever it was disappeared before she could decipher it.

"Now for the camera?" Alessio gestured toward the media gear.

Brie opened her mouth. Of course the moment wasn't momentous for him. It was only her first kiss after all, a prep for the real show.

"Now for the camera." Brie smiled, hoping it looked real.

CHAPTER FOUR

BRIE'S HEAD WAS buried in her phone as she lifted what he suspected was at least her second cup of coffee. She made a few notes on the small notebook beside her, a frown crossing her lips.

"What's wrong?"

Brie looked up, her eyes widening as she met his gaze. "When did you get here?"

"Not long ago, but you were focused."

When he was in his glass shop, people had been able to sneak up on him. He'd get lost in the moment, in the creative juices that flowed when he was working on a piece.

"You frowned. So I repeat, what's wrong?"

"Our second kiss looked too stilted. The feedback on the story I put up is less than stellar. There are comments that we look like robots."

"Oh." Alessio slid into the chair next to her. "I take it that is bad." He'd known that the second kiss was lacking, especially compared to the first.

The first. The feel of her lips on his, her body molding to his. It was magic, a kiss like he'd never experienced. He'd wanted to melt into her, spend the rest of the night worshipping her lips. Then she'd joked that they should have filmed that one.

A nervous joke. He'd understood that immediately, but it had stolen the illusion from the moment. Their second kiss, the one she'd uploaded, felt much more like two strangers—which they were.

"Yes. It's bad." Brie downed the rest of her coffee, hopped off the chair and filled her cup again. "But we're marketing Celiana. Not us." Brie blew out a breath. "Love is boring."

"Really?" Everything about the Princess Lottery seemed to indicate otherwise.

"Yes." Brie sighed like it should be obvious. "It's why your parents' love story never really made headlines."

Love story.

It was weird to hear that knowing it was false. "Their wedding kept the honeymoon industry going. That is the legacy of their love."

"No." Brie slid back into her seat. Her jeweled gaze caught his.

His breath skipped. She was so close, the aroma of her coffee and the sweet scent that was just Brie reminded him of their kiss. Their first one.

"Their legacy is the wedding." Brie shrugged, like she wasn't just dismissing the mythos of the great love the palace carefully sculpted.

Before he could add to that, she continued, "Your father had no identified mistresses."

Only the country.

"Your mother was faithful, too. Delivering an heir and…"

A blush invaded her cheeks as she looked away. "And a spare."

The word didn't matter to him. He'd heard it his entire life. He was the spare. The one that really only mattered if something happened to his brother. It was a scenario Alessio never wanted to happen.

Brie's hand closed over his. "The point I'm trying to make—" she squeezed him and for a moment he thought she'd let him go, but instead she kept holding his hand "—is that gossip is more fun. Love—true love—is boring. Aka your parents."

She blew out a breath. "I don't know how we fake that, though. We need to be boring so they focus in on the locations."

"I do." Alessio lifted her hand, kissing the center. It was a sweet gesture, one he'd seen his father do a million times with his mother.

"That is a Prince Charming move." Brie sighed. "But I am serious."

"I know." Alessio took a deep breath. "You can't tell anyone what I am about to say."

Brie nodded.

"My parents weren't in love."

Her mouth fell open, but he didn't wait for the exclamation he saw building.

"It was an act. A well-scripted one. They cared for each other, but it wasn't love—not really." Alessio knew he was rambling, but he wanted her to understand. "They caressed a lot in front of reporters when they were first wed—at least that's what I've heard. Once the story was set, they lessened the touches, but people just figured it was normal longtime married-couple things."

Alessio ran his thumb along her palm, grateful she was still holding him. It was weird to talk with an outsider about this. "I know it sounds bad. And I know they respected each other, but behind the palace walls, they lived independent lives."

"That is perfect!"

Perfect. Not exactly the response Alessio expected. Or wanted.

"So we pattern ourselves after your parents. We act like they did. Happy is not fun to discuss."

He understood that. At the heart of the show, he'd always heard not to frown, not to make a face. A face could be interpreted, and the interpretation was always the thing that sold the story.

"So for our hike up the falls today—" Alessio looked at her hands, ones he'd need to hold, to kiss, to touch "—we act like we are falling in love."

The path to freedom wouldn't be difficult to walk. But the idea of role-playing love with Brie sent an uncomfortable arrow through his heart.

"And in the palace, we can lead separate lives for the next few weeks." She looked down and ran her hand along the back of her neck.

Then she grabbed her phone. That thing was an extension of her. "Shall we try a little live? It's early still, so we won't have as many viewers, which might make us looser."

"Sure." Alessio shrugged. "But what are we going to talk about?"

Brie bit her lip, then shook her head. "Let's run it without a script. A 'get to know you live' kind of thing. My family is off-limits. So is yours. Any other questions unwelcome?"

"I don't discuss the years I was away."

Brie nodded. "Understood. Though I'll admit that I am a little desperate to know. The only trips I took out of the kingdom were with my family, and I spent far too much of those vacations with a book in a boardroom while Dad had a meeting he couldn't—or didn't want to—reschedule. Not information I'd planned to share. And that right there is why we put things off the table."

Brie laughed and let her hand graze his knee. She set up the phone on a stack of books she must have carted down from the media room, and he watched her slide into "on" mode. Her shoulders were just a little straighter, her smile a little too full. But then he had an "on" side, too. One he needed to get into.

"Good morning, Celiana." Brie waved before holding up her coffee cup. "Alessio and I are in the kitchen, having coffee, and thought we'd spend a little time with you."

She leaned closer, making sure they were both in the frame. His arm slid around the back of her chair, and he could tell it pleased her.

After all, it looked good for the camera, though he'd done it to make sure she didn't tumble out of the tall chair. It was an unrealistic fear, but his body had acted without thinking.

She lifted the coffee cup again.

"How many cups of coffee have you had this

morning?" Alessio winked before making eye contact with the phone. Was he supposed to talk to her or them? That was a question he should have asked.

"More than one, less than—" Brie put a finger on her chin "—less than six."

"Five cups, Brie!"

She grinned and her look was so infectious he nearly forgot about the camera.

"In my defense, your cups are small." She held up what looked like a regular coffee cup to him.

"If you think about it, it's unfair to judge by this tiny thing." She set it down and leaned on the counter. "I should have thought to grab one of my coffee mugs."

"I fail to see how the size of the mug impacts the amount of coffee you drink." He reached his hands across the island, letting his fingers wrap with hers.

Touching her was intoxicating, and they'd agreed that they needed to look affectionate. It should feel like acting…at least a little. Yet…it felt so natural as her fingers linked with his.

"It's the same amount by volume." She made a silly face, then stuck her tongue out at the "tiny" mug. "But then I can say that I drank two cups, and it sounds less horrendous."

"How big is your mug?"

Brie threw her free hand over her face, the drama making him chuckle. "There is no mug big enough. But mine holds basically half a pot." She beamed, then looked at the phone. "Next topic. Are you ready for our hike?"

"Sure."

He'd hiked the Falls of Oneiros several times as a child. The area was beautiful, but he hadn't visited in years.

"The Falls of Dreams." Brie sighed and pulled her hand away. "My brother, Beau, and I used to stand at the top, think of our dreams and throw a petal over the falls."

She bit her lip then lifted the cup. Family was supposed to be off-limits. Beau Ailiono was a business scion, the heir to the Ailiono fortune, but he and Brie had been close enough once to hike and wish for something at the falls.

It was the standard routine at the falls. Oneiros, Greek for *dreams*, was where the locals came to cast wishes. Few tourists found their way there.

That would change once they visited—hopefully. The tourism industry had not courted the outdoorsy types. She was right; they had restricted their focus, and opening that up was a good thing.

Though he wasn't sure it would be enough.

"What were your dreams?"

He and his brother had never participated in making wishes when they'd hiked the falls. Their lives were planned out. The expectations known. What good were dreams when the path was already set in stone before you?

What had she thought was possible? What had she wanted more than anything?

"Freedom." She cleared her throat.

He did not know what to say to that. Freedom.

His heart clenched as he stared at her wavering smile. Freedom. One word, with so much meaning.

Freedom was something royal life did not allow.

"What were yours?"

The question interrupted his worries. At least he had an easy answer. "I never made a wish."

He felt the weight of her stare, but what was there to say? His role was determined from the moment of his birth. To wish for more... Well, that had led to the greatest heartbreak of his life: closing his shop and returning home.

"Well. That changes today!" Brie waved at the camera. "Who wants to see Alessio toss a petal?"

A ton of hearts and comments saying "Yes!" flooded the chat screen.

"All right, stay tuned." Brie leaned over and kissed his cheek, then shut the live stream off.

"Was that better?"

"Yes." Brie tilted her head, thoughts clearly evident in her eyes.

Sadness or pity? He wasn't sure, but he didn't like either option.

"You are more than the title prince."

Whatever he'd expected her to say, that wasn't it.

"Not really." He finished his cup of coffee and left the chair. Once upon a time he'd been more than the spare. More than a prince. He wanted to believe it was possible for it to happen again, but the odds… He didn't even want to calculate them.

Freedom.

The word echoed in his mind.

"You are more than your title, Alessio."

"Well." He stepped around the kitchen island and pulled her into his arms. "I am a fiancé now, too."

"I'm serious, Alessio." Brie's hands cupped the sides of his face.

He could tell she'd done it impulsively, but he enjoyed her touch. A little too much.

This didn't feel like living separate lives when her phone's camera wasn't on—when no one was looking. It felt real, and far more terrifying.

"Fine. I'm more than my title."

"Good." Brie released him, her gaze following her hands before she crossed her arms. "Now… um…" She looked over her shoulder. "I need to get ready for the hike. Good job this morning."

He playfully offered a military salute. If she saw the humor in his movements, she didn't react. And then she was gone.

"I guess people got the message…"

Brie stared out the window of the SUV. The crowd was at least three people deep even though they'd blocked the hiking path off and they had a three-hour window to hike on their own. She'd pushed for an open hike; the palace security team hadn't laughed in her face, but they'd squashed the idea with exceptional speed.

However, she didn't mind spending time alone with Alessio as she should. This morning they'd said they needed to look happy, like they were falling in love. That was the method his parents had used—so successfully that she'd had no idea. But her touches for the camera were the ones that felt off, unlike touching his knee over coffee or when she'd put her hands on either side of his face; those felt so real.

And for a moment today, she'd seen herself, felt the connection between them that was more than the lottery. She'd worn the same look as him once.

The Ailiono daughter. A piece on her family's chessboard. She'd seen the same despair when he said he wasn't more than his title. She'd still have that feeling if she hadn't left her family.

If she married Alessio, would she experience the same desperation again? Yes. It was why she needed her freedom. But after seeing his look this morning, she needed freedom for him, too. Alessio was far more than his title. He wasn't the spare, the heir only until his brother married and had children. From this point forward she'd focus on the man, not the title.

"The message you broadcast?" Alessio's hand tapped her knee. "Yes, I think that message got out."

He pulled his hand away. Technically no one could see them yet, but part of her wished he'd left it.

"True." Brie knew the crowd was here for the

lottery princess, here for the story, but it was weird to see so many people. People normally avoided the Ailiono family—unless they were hoping to make money with them.

No one would describe the Ailiono family as easy to be around. Beau had been, *once*. Then he became their father's mini-me, the man set to take over the Ailiono family dynasty.

He'd abandoned her. She'd hoped he might ride to her rescue when she was unceremoniously kicked out. She'd held out hope for far too long that he might show up.

She shook the memory from her head. Beau was the perfect Ailiono family member. She wasn't. So their paths had parted.

Had Alessio and Sebastian had a good relationship growing up? What happened when Alessio left? Those were questions she couldn't ask him, though Brie was curious. Deep down, she knew they'd experienced some of the same trauma. And they craved the same thing.

He kissed the top of her head. They'd agreed they needed to touch, needed to make it look real for the camera. Her plan wouldn't work unless people focused on the recreational sites Celiana offered. That meant they couldn't give the likes of journalists like Lev things to feed into rumors of unhappiness.

People liked a love story…they loved a disaster. That was the real public relations rule. If they looked unhappy, it wouldn't matter where they went. All the world would see were the frowns.

But she didn't want him to kiss her forehead. She wanted him to kiss her lips. Their first kiss had poured through her far longer than the few minutes her lips had touched his. It was an ugly reminder of how much the second kiss was lacking.

She'd thought about that first kiss far too much, which was acceptable if she was a blushing schoolgirl. But as a twenty-six-year-old woman…

"Let's do this. Your smile ready?"

This needed to look good. Tourists were on vacation. Vacation was happy time.

"I can always find a smile." Alessio grinned, but it was the prince smile, one she might not have fully pegged as fake until she'd spent time with him. But now it was easy to see; if she could see it, so might others, too.

"We need authentic smiles."

Alessio's brows rose before he pursed his lips. "It is a real smile."

"No." Brie shook her head. "It's Prince Charming out for an outing. It's not real."

"Prince Charming is a fantasy. I am no fantasy." Alessio leaned closer to her, his lips spreading into a convincing smile.

Brie held up her hands, pretending they were a camera. "Click." She laughed as his head tilted, his grin growing even bigger. "That was a genuine smile. Focus on whatever brought that out."

"You brought it out." Alessio pulled on the back of his neck as he turned his attention to the crowd.

She knew those words had slipped out unintentionally, but her insides warmed as she watched the smile on his lips. She'd done that. It was silly to care about, but still...

"Luckily for you, I will be on the trail beside you the whole time." Brie blew out a breath and grabbed the door handle. "Showtime!"

"Briella! Princess Briella!"

"Princess!"

"Briella!"

The calls rose around her. Flashes from cameras and held-up cell phones, which she knew were recording, greeted them on the side of the path. There were makeshift barriers with lots of people stood behind them.

She'd wanted an audience; her plan depended on it. But it was still a lot to take in.

Alessio squeezed her hand as they wandered to the barrier. His smile looked genuine, full, and it eased her as she stepped into the role, too.

Alessio started shaking hands, and Brie smiled at a young girl.

"You're such a pretty princess." The girl held up a sunflower.

Brie bent down so she could meet the girl's eyes.

"I'm not a princess…not yet. Just Brie. What's your name?"

"Ella. Like the end of your name. My mom owns a bakery. It's always busy now. She said last night that it was because of you."

A woman standing behind Ella let out a soft groan. "I've told you not to eavesdrop on Daddy and I. Give her the flower, honey."

Ella looked at her mother and made a face. "But I want her to know the rest."

"Know what?" Brie asked, making sure she kept a serious face. Ella was serious, and Brie could be serious, too, though a laugh was bubbling in her chest.

"I like to play Cinderella, but now I can play Princess Briella." Her smile was so wide, so open.

Brie looked to Ella's mother. The woman had taken time out of her bakery to come with her daughter today. The country needed the tourists; family bakeries thrived on them. But the hope in Ella's and her mother's eyes sent fear tumbling through her. What if Brie's plan failed?

Ella and her mother weren't the only regular people here. Yes, the press was here, but so were many regular folks whose livelihoods were riding on Prince Alessio and Princess Briella.

Brie looked at Alessio. His gaze met hers, and he grinned before turning back to the gathered crowd. She'd sworn to meet him at the altar if her plan failed, but she'd refused to think of the possibility. And she couldn't focus on it now.

"Thank you for the flower, Ella."

Alessio placed a hand on her shoulder, and she rose. "If we want to hike the trail before the day gets too warm, we should get moving."

"Agreed." Brie smiled at the crowd, though now she suspected it was her smile looking forced instead of Alessio's.

She took his hand, her body relaxing a little with the touch, waved with the sunflower, then followed him down the path.

"I think we did pretty well there." Alessio adjusted his backpack as they started up the trailhead.

"I think so, too."

At the very least, it was a good start. The actual test happened with the video they did at the falls. Could they successfully turn the attention to the falls and not them?

"And now we hike." Alessio pulled one arm in front of him, stretching his shoulder, then did the other.

"Now we hike," Brie conceded. The trip to the falls would take about an hour. In silence it would seem like forever. "So maybe we should play twenty questions."

"Twenty questions? What is that?"

Brie shook her head. "Seriously, Prince Charming? It's exactly what it sounds like. You ask each other twenty questions, 'get to know you' style. I'll start. Favorite color?"

"Green. You?"

"Light blue. Like the water over the falls. Favorite season?"

"Summer."

They continued the questions as they walked the path. The questions were getting a little deeper but carefully avoiding anything too deep.

"Who was your first fiancé?"

She lost her footing, and Alessio's hand caught her elbow. His eyes locked with hers as he steadied her.

"Brie?"

That was not a question she'd expected.

"Sorry. Maybe I shouldn't have asked, but I assume he is not a security threat. Or is it possible he is?"

Security was important for the royal family, but she didn't think that was why Alessio was asking.

The fiancé… That was the night she'd broken with her family forever after refusing to play the role they'd carefully planned out for her. The role her mother played for her father, despite how unhappy it made her.

Kate Ailiono was the "perfect wife."

In public. Behind closed doors, *shrew* was the kindest word one could say. She was jealous of the mistresses and time spent away from the family home. The screaming matches were epic.

The only problem was Brie, and that she wasn't willing to follow in her mother's footsteps.

Time slowed as they stood together on the path. Alessio wrapped an arm around her waist as they looked over a mountain pass. Her past and the future were slamming together. Except he wasn't her future.

She never talked about Milo Friollo. Ophelia only knew because she'd helped Brie escape the Ailiono compound the night her father announced the union.

She could still visualize the man sitting beside her at the table. Milo had smiled and reached out to hold her hand. No notice had been given to her. There was no expectation that she'd do anything other than follow.

"Forget I asked. What was the last book you read?" His tone was sweet, but she could hear the bead of worry under it.

Her most recent read was on marketing to different Enneagram types. She could tell him that and ignore the other question. That was the simple answer, but she couldn't quite find the words.

Brie reached for Alessio's hand and started back up the trail.

"I never talk about him."

The sentence slipped into the open. His name burned the back of her throat, but she didn't say it. Alessio walked beside her but said nothing. No questions, no pressure.

Pressure was an Ailiono family specialty. No one could make silence hurt like her family.

And yet, she'd nearly gone back—so many times. When her feet were bleeding from standing for hours as a barista with burns on her hands, and her eyes were so heavy from exhaustion as she tried to study and keep a tiny roof over her head, she'd thought of it. On her birthday, when no card, no phone call, no acknowledgment from her family came, the desire to belong again had nearly driven her home. When her rent was due and she was short… When everyone was out at bars, having fun, and she was skipping meals…

"Milo was older." That was a kind statement. The man was three times her age, a lifetime of lived experiences to her teenage self.

"Milo Friollo?"

That Alessio could guess at the man her parents had arranged for her wasn't surprising. Milo walked down the aisle more than most. And each wife was younger than the last. He'd married six months after that dinner. And there'd been another last year—wife four was nineteen…just like Brie had been.

"My father and he are business partners. Or they were. I'm not sure their professional relationship survived my flight. Though it probably did. Money is what matters after all."

Once the words were out, her brain refused to stop. "They ambushed me at a family dinner. Announced that we'd marry in six months." Her fingers flexed as the memory of Milo's touch echoed in her brain. "He married another on our wedding date. Though that union lasted less than a year."

"Ambushed?" Alessio let out a grunt.

"It's not that different from the countless other marriages made for prestige, family alliances or money. People like to pretend that we are so different from our historical counterparts, but the truth is the wealthy and privileged rarely marry for love.

"Hell, we are trying to get out of a nearly iron-clad marriage contract." Brie laughed. There had to be humor, or she'd cry. "They disowned me for refusing to follow my parents' demands and somehow I ended up back in an arranged marriage." The laughter died away.

"I hope you get out." His words were barely audible.

"You hope I get out. What about you? If you could be anywhere, where would it be?"

"I don't know."

"I think you do." The heat in Brie's cheeks had nothing to do with the hike. She'd answered the one personal question he'd asked, but it appeared that he would not do the same.

They hiked the rest of the trail in silence.

"The falls!" She raised her hand, pointing to the crystal blue water cascading over the mountain's edge. The Falls of Oneiros.

The Falls of Dreams.

"It's gorgeous." Alessio let out a breath as he followed her gaze.

His lack of response to her question frustrated her, but she also wanted him to have this moment, a real one, before she turned on the camera. She grabbed two petals and pressed one into his hand as they moved to stand as close to the edge as possible.

"Do you need to get the phone out?" Alessio looked at the petal like it might bite.

"No. Not for your first wish. We'll film another, but this one… I don't know, it's tradition. You should get to do it the way everyone else does."

"Sebastian and I always knew our roles. Heir and spare—what good were wishes?"

The words broke her heart. Family expectations were hard, but he'd had expectations from the country, too.

"Make a wish. There has to be something you crave."

A look passed over his eyes and Brie lifted up on her toes. It wasn't planned, and there was still frustration bubbling in her. But she was drawn to him. She pressed her lips to his. His arms wrapped around her waist. Alessio deepened the kiss.

The mountain hummed in sync with the racing falls. The world seemed to cheer their connection.

Here and now, there was only her and Alessio. The security team had cleared the falls before they arrived and was standing down the trail, around a bend. In this moment it would be easy to pretend this was a regular date. He was a man who just wanted to spend time with Brie.

It would be easy to pretend they'd met somewhere and were regular people with regular expectations.

But pretending wouldn't get her what she wanted, the freedom she craved. Pulling back, she held up her petal.

"Ready?" She winked and gestured for him to hold up his, too.

He looked at his petal and she could see words

tumbling in his eyes. A want, something buried so deep.

"Here, I'll show you how." She held the petal to her chest.

Freedom. It was the word she'd always thought when she stood here. *Freedom.*

She let the petal loose and opened her eyes to watch it float over the falls.

"Your turn." She reached for his free hand. "Close your eyes."

Alessio looked at her, then closed his eyes.

"Lift the petal to your chest and think about what you want. What you really want, Alessio."

He did as she said, taking a deep breath.

"Now let it go."

He opened his palm, and the petal floated into the falls. He opened his eyes and wrapped his arm around her waist. She didn't think as she laid her head against his shoulder.

"See, that wasn't so hard, was it?"

His lips brushed her head. "Thank you for the experience, Brie."

Again they stood in silence. Finally, he squeezed her. "Scotland. If I could go anywhere, it would be Scotland."

Before she could ask any follow-ups, Alessio grabbed two more petals. "Now, showtime."

"Right." She'd nearly forgotten. She'd been lost in the moments of his kiss, in him.

It was good that he'd reminded her... It didn't sting. Not even a little bit.

CHAPTER FIVE

ALESSIO LOOKED AT his watch. He'd gotten a quick swim in after dinner and had the rest of the evening to himself. Brie would be in the media room. It was where she spent any free time. And today there'd been quite a lot of freedom.

Which meant he'd not seen her much.

They'd enjoyed a quick outing at a local bakery. The small trip was designed to give the illusion of dating while highlighting a local establishment. They'd stayed less than an hour, and talked to the baker and her son. He'd eaten a few cookies. Brie had—

Alessio closed his eyes. He'd been so focused on the discussion that he wasn't sure she'd sampled anything. He stopped, his mind flashing to the first day—how was that less than a week ago? She'd looked like a deer in headlights by the dessert plate.

Her mother was notorious for controlling what food passed her lips. The comments Brie's mother made to the ladies and men of the court were often downright rude. If that was what she was willing to say in public, what vitriol had Brie heard behind closed doors?

It wasn't hard to imagine. His father had leveled complaints against him at every chance. Though never about food.

It was nearly seven. That meant that if she'd grabbed dinner, she was bent over spreadsheets and crunching data that seemed to appear from nowhere.

She wouldn't look for him for the rest of the night. They were in the palace. That meant separate spheres. She hadn't wanted to put up a video about them this evening. Instead, she was tracking what people were saying about the visit to the Falls of Oneiros two days ago and the bakery this morning.

They each wanted this to succeed, but she needed a break, too. And he had an idea that might just work. It would only take a few minutes to put it together.

He knocked on the door, waited for her call to enter, then swept the door open and pushed in the cart the kitchen staff had helped him prepare.

"What?" Brie's hair was falling out of her bun and there were smudges on the glasses she wore when working at the computer. Her oversize sweater easily fit over her knees, which she had pulled up in her chair.

"Good evening, Brie."

She looked at the tray he was pushing and raised a brow. "Good evening. I…um… I already ate."

He knew that. The kitchen staff had told him she'd gotten a chicken salad sandwich and some veggies. But no dessert.

Alessio walked over to the desk and nearly leaned in to kiss her cheek. They were in the palace. The little touches weren't needed, but that didn't stop him from wanting them.

Brie's gaze focused on his lips. Had she wanted him to kiss her?

Kissing was not the purpose of this encounter. He honestly wasn't entirely sure what this was about, but he'd wanted to spend time with her.

"I know you ate, but this isn't dinner." Her brow raised again. "Figure you gave me something special the other day, so I'm hoping to return the favor."

"Something special?" A frown touched her lips, and he wanted to wipe it away. "A wish isn't something special, Alessio."

"Why?" He walked to the cart and pushed it by the little table she used for meals before gesturing for her to join him. This wasn't a grand affair, but he wanted her to enjoy it away from spreadsheets and numbers.

She bit her lip as she walked over and looked at the covered trays.

"Because mine was staged. I think it is important that you made a wish. You are more than a prince. You get to have your own dreams and wishes, but…"

Brie hesitated and looked at her feet. She sucked in a deep breath, then looked back at him. "But mine was for the show."

"Not the first one." He squeezed her hand, then lifted it to his lips.

"Yes, but—"

"But nothing. My first wish was mine. So little in my life is." The wish was a moment, one he got to hold deep in his soul even if he doubted it could come true.

"But now…" He pulled off the covers of the two trays with what he hoped was a flourish.

"Cookies and pie." She let out a laugh. "Not sure what I expected, but somehow sweets wasn't it."

His stomach twisted. What else might be under such a display? The Ailiono family was notorious for controlling business dealings, but it was clear Brie had been controlled in other ways. And she'd escaped.

She'd made her own way, only to find herself behind the bars of another cage.

"I know your mother doesn't like sweets."

Her laughter was bitter as it echoed against the walls. "My mother abhors treats. Anything that might add a pinch of weight to her waistline."

"Her waistline…" Alessio leaned forward on his hands. "And yours?"

"Ailiono children are extensions of their parents. Beau is my father, even if once upon a time I thought he might break away. Thought he might come with me, but…well…he didn't."

There was more to that story. But Brie cleared her throat as she picked up a cookie. Her eyes didn't move from the raspberry lemon one.

"I was my mother."

"Was." Alessio reached for her hand. "You *were*, but now you are Brie, Princess of Celiana, eater of whatever sweets she chooses!"

"Princess?" Brie pushed at his shoulder. "Alessio. I know you're joking, but it is so weird to hear 'Princess Brie.' Even after crowds have shouted it for days."

She was stalling. So he grabbed the other raspberry lemon cookie. He popped the tiny pastry in his mouth. The flavors were divine.

"Your turn."

Brie looked at the cookie, then up at him. If she pushed back, he'd stop, but he wanted her to try. She squeezed his hand then took a small bite. A tiny bite in a tiny cookie, but a bite.

"Thoughts?"

"It's tart. Fine."

"*Fine* is not what we are looking for!" He grabbed a dark chocolate bar and passed it to her. Chocolate was his mother's favorite. He preferred fruit flavors.

She took a bite and then another. "All right. That *is* good."

Chocolate made her smile. Good to know!

She lifted the lavender cookie from the tin. "This looks too pretty to eat." Turning the cookie, she pointed to the small lavender outline the baker had created in the center.

"A work of art." He grabbed its twin. "That is designed to be eaten."

"Art shouldn't be eaten."

"No. This art should. Art is designed to give the person near it a feeling, an experience. A painting might bring out happiness or sorrow. A sculpture may remind you of a loved one who passed or a brilliant childhood memory. And cookies, pastries, they are designed to evoke the majesty of the flavors. It does the baker a disservice to think it too pretty to eat."

"Wow. What is your creative outlet?"

Brie's jeweled gaze captured him. Expectation and happiness were bright as she guessed at what was truly in his soul.

"What?"

Brie set the cookie down. "What is your thing? Painting? Sculpture? Did you make the cookie?"

"No." He'd not meant to let so much out, but the words could be of an art aficionado, not an artist. He was a patron of Celiana's art scene. Even the Princess Lottery was a fundraiser for it.

Her hands wrapped around his waist, her sweet scent lighting through him. "Come on, Alessio. No one talks that passionately about art without doing something."

"Lots of people talk about art passionately."

They did. He'd stood in many a gallery with people who'd never picked up a brush but waxed on about the meaning of a piece.

"I'm sure they do. But not with the feeling you had in your voice or the twinkle in their eye. Are you a mime?"

"A mime?"

Brie pulled back, a giggle in her eyes. "Sure. That's an art form. What's yours?"

No one had ever just asked him what his creative outlet was. No one had even guessed the prince had one. In his glass studio, covered in sweat from the fires and dust from the shop, he'd looked less than regal. But he'd been happy.

"Glasswork."

"Oh. Like melting glass and bending it." Brie tilted her head, and he could see all the questions building.

Alessio nodded. "It's a little more but yes, at its base, it's melting and bending."

At his height in the shop, he'd made a few pieces a day. Most of them sold, and he had a few in his suite that he couldn't part with.

"You have to show me."

"Can't. I gave it up. Princely duties and all." There was a workshop on the palace grounds. It was his workshop. But the glass ball he'd made for the lottery was his final piece, his goodbye to the art as he stepped into the role he'd been born to play.

"That's a shame." She stuck her bottom lip out, then opened her mouth but closed it without saying whatever had come to her mind.

She put the whole tiny cookie in her mouth, closed her eyes and let out the softest sigh. He wasn't sure exactly what Brie was experiencing, but watching her was magical.

"That is divine."

"You're divine." The words slipped out, but he didn't want to pull them back. She was perfection.

Brie looked at him, and he nearly shifted as she seemed to stare right into his soul.

The world with its requirements, its worries, the concerns for the kingdom and Brie's plans—it all vanished as she dropped a quick kiss on his cheek.

"Um…" She looked at him, and he could see the shock running through her face.

She'd not planned to kiss him. It wasn't on the schedule after all.

His hands moved without thinking, pulling her back into his arms. She sighed, like there was no other place she'd rather be, then lifted her head. Their lips met and once more the world seemed to stand still.

She tasted like chocolate and freedom, and he craved every piece of her. Her fingers moved along his back, her body pressing against his. Every sense was tuned to Brie.

Brie stepped back and he let her go, even though the urge to deepen the kiss, to run his fingers over her bare skin, was crying out within him.

Her cheeks were a delicate rose as she pointed to the trays. "Chocolate. I like chocolate. The lavender is good, too. I mean, even the lemon raspberry was good."

They were shifting topics. That was probably for the best. "You don't have to lie. You didn't like it."

Brie pursed her lips and pushed a piece of hair behind her ear. "It was all right...nothing like chocolate, though."

"So we start trying out different chocolates for dessert."

If she wanted to shift the conversation away from kisses, he'd go with the flow. She'd lacked control before. There were parts of their lives that would always be out of their control, but Alessio would give her as much as possible.

"Chocolate flavors? How many flavors are there?"

"More than I can count." He wrapped an arm around her shoulder, not really intending to, but his heart skipped as she laid her head on his shoulder.

"Dessert is nice. No wonder my mother wanted me to avoid it." Brie sat up, the past breaking through the illusion of the treats.

"I wanted to show you the metrics I have. The falls have seen a large booking, and the bakery sold out. Of course, we won't have all the metrics for several more weeks. Still, the focus of the first few adventures has stayed on the location after brief mentions of us...touching."

The hesitation caught his attention, but she was

already throwing things up on the smart board. Tables, charts, growth exports—all were very impressive, he thought.

He'd done his time in economics and stats classes, getting through on pure grit with a barely passing grade. Most of the time he'd spent in those classes was daydreaming ways to sculpt whatever creation was burning through his mind.

King Cedric hadn't allowed Alessio to major in art or art history. That was not a proper "princely" topic, according to the king. That hadn't stopped Alessio from spending all of his free time with the art teacher and master glassworker.

"Do you ever tire of it? Of the cameras? The questions?" Brie's questions roused his mind from trying to make sense of the numbers before him.

"No."

She spun around, horror clear on her face. "Come on, Alessio. Never? You were the rebel once upon a time. The skipper of as many engagements as possible. The royal who stuck his tongue out instead of answering pointed questions. You really never tire of it now? Of the lack of privacy? Of the rules? The regulations? The stares…the…"

He caught her fingers, holding them tightly, grounding himself in the present. Once upon a time, he'd rebelled against everything. He'd hated the cameras, the lack of privacy. Giving in to those emotions again might be cathartic, but if this effort failed… Alessio wasn't willing to hope yet.

"When I returned, I pledged myself to Celiana."

A look passed across her features. It sent a shiver through his soul. It would be her life, too, should they meet at the altar.

"It's not a horror show, Brie." He squeezed her fingers.

"It's not *not* a horror show."

That was hard to argue with. "I guess I just see it as part of the duty. Just an extension of the crown."

"Dutiful Alessio. Why the change?"

"It was time to grow up."

She pulled her fingers back, and he watched the wall crash back down between them. The openness was closing as she flipped back to her spreadsheets.

Brie could tell when he wasn't fully honest. She was the only one bothered by his surface-level answers. She was also the only one that paid close enough attention to tell the difference. Brie deserved the answer, but he couldn't give it.

It was cowardly, but that was a story he wasn't going to share with anyone. Even Sebastian didn't know the real reason he'd returned. That secret was buried with his father and that was where it was staying.

CHAPTER SIX

BRIE BIT HER lip as she looked at the email, then looked to the door. Alessio would be here any moment for breakfast. Despite saying they wouldn't spend time together in the palace, they took all their meals together now. And if he saw her frowning, he'd worry and ask why. And she'd probably tell him.

That wouldn't be a big deal if he was telling her personal things. Like what was in Scotland—or who. Or why he'd come home to stay. He could have come for the funeral and then headed back—right?

Brie let out a sigh. She wasn't actually clear on what the rules were for the heir. Maybe he'd had to return and stay. But that didn't mean he had to give up glassworking.

She'd wanted an answer but he'd refused to discuss it or give a full explanation. He was holding back. And if Alessio wasn't opening up fully, then neither was she.

Her business was precious, and this was the second possible cancellation this week for a job she'd scheduled before her name had echoed across the kingdom two weeks ago.

Fourteen days and a lifetime all at once.

The first week, two cancellations had come in saying they wished her well on this endeavor, but understood that her new duties would mean diminished time for their accounts. The email on Monday had asked if she planned to complete the jobs scheduled. It was polite, but they'd included all the account information to return their retainer.

And now this email was here. Yes, no princess in the history of Celiana had worked outside the palace. But she didn't plan to be a princess.

The stats were still up, though not as much as she was hoping to see. It had only been two weeks. That was a blip in marketing time. But with the viral marketing campaign she'd developed, she'd expected more. Or maybe she was just hoping for more. And there were pockets of dissent already, comments that they'd done nothing "wedding" related.

No bridal gown shopping. No cake testing. No venue discussions.

Two weeks. They'd been "engaged" two weeks. It wasn't like all couples immediately hopped to planning. Still, a rumor could tank this whole thing, so she'd scheduled a wedding outing to calm the waters before the ripple fully developed.

Tapping her fingers, she tried to bring her focus back to this problem. If she sent back the retainer for this job, that would mean she'd lost four jobs— so far. She blinked back the tears that were threatening. She'd built her business from nothing once. Brie could do it again.

If she had to.

Taking a deep breath, she typed out the reply thanking them for reaching out and offering to return the retainer, then deleted it. Instead, she sent a quick line saying that, while she was busy, she fully intended to fulfill all her contracts. She'd planned to take a few weeks off following the bride lottery anyway, so nothing was disrupted. She'd be in touch at the beginning of next month and let them know they were at the top of her calendar.

By then she and Alessio would be laying the groundwork for the breakup anyway.

The thought tore through her. Breakup.

This isn't real, Brie. It's not a breakup. Not really.

So why did the thought of not seeing him again bother her so?

Her mind drifted to how he kissed, how his lips felt as they brushed hers, how he tasted when she deepened the kiss.

Then her mind took it a step further. She dreamed of how his fingers tracing down her skin might feel, dreamed of his lips finding far more than her mouth.

Pushing away from the computer, she wandered to the smart board and looked at the graphs she'd developed for the latest outings. She needed to focus on those, not on the handsome prince always by her side, despite their initial pledge to not spend time together inside the palace.

The door opened, and she couldn't stop the smile as Alessio stepped in—juggling two cups of coffee.

"Good morning." He handed her a cup, and she saw his eyes flit to the pot in the corner. "Not sure I should aid in your caffeine intake."

Over the last week, he'd told her that a walk outside or a swim in the pool would be just as good a way to wake herself up. She'd visited him at the pool once. And him in a bathing suit had definitely woken something in her.

"I've only had one…no, two." She thought hard. "Yes, only two so far."

"Only." Alessio shook his head before dropping a kiss on her cheek. "You all right? You look a little off this morning."

Little got past him. It was sweet and unnerving.

Her family had never noticed little things about her. And her coffee habit was not a little thing. She'd used caffeine to keep herself up since she was in high school. It was a habit her parents hadn't minded.

Her parents felt the same way about work as Alessio did now about duty. It was what you did. To question that was unthinkable.

"Breakfast for the princess and prince. Celiana's lovers," Sebastian sang as he strolled through the door with a bag of something he tossed to Alessio.

"Muffins?"

"Homemade!" He winked as he slid onto the couch.

Alessio looked at the bag and frowned. "In other words, you slipped your security team, spent the night with a woman and left before she woke?"

"Alessio—" Brie's voice was soft as she stepped to his side.

"No need to fret, Princess." Sebastian let out a soft laugh. "This is a common refrain we share. Unlike my brother, I waited until dear old Dad passed to learn how to slip my security detail. You should try it again, brother."

Alessio's body went rigid beside her, and she heard the bag crumple in his fingers before he handed it to her, the top of it nearly mangled.

"You are the king."

The words slipped from her lips before she'd thought them through. This wasn't her fight, but Alessio's brow was furrowed. He'd clenched and unclenched his palm three times and was fighting to keep from shifting on his feet.

How quickly she'd learned his little tells over the last weeks. She wanted to wipe away the worry. But she also understood Sebastian's need for freedom.

She'd craved it for so long, come so close to it. Surely Alessio understood, too.

"Thank you. Exactly." Alessio wrapped his arm around her waist, grounding himself as he stood just a hair taller.

"Wow, the lovers are teaming up. Interesting."

"Don't change the subject, Sebastian. What happens if something happens to you?"

Alessio shifted his feet and Brie thought he wanted to stomp them but was resisting. Was that a hint of the rebel pushing out?

"You have security for a reason," Alessio stated. "If something happens, you can handle it. The man that returned to the island is quite dutiful." Sebastian closed his eyes and leaned his head against the couch's back. "Perhaps that is a win for everyone."

"No." Alessio's voice echoed through the room.

"Because you don't want the damn throne, either. Don't want everyone wanting you for the crown."

"Because I don't want to lose you." Alessio was vibrating.

"Weird statement, considering you were the one that abandoned the family. Didn't care if we lived or died then."

"Damn it, Sebastian. That is not—" His eyes flicked to Brie.

She saw him bite back whatever it was he planned to say.

Brie reached for him as he stepped away from her. "Alessio—"

"Excuse me, sweetheart. I need a moment. I'll see you shortly." He turned, closing the door softly.

"It would have been more dramatic to slam the door." Sebastian clicked his tongue. "Not that my brother would ever do such a thing. At least not now. He used to do it as an art form. When he ran away to Scotland, the door he slammed nearly came off its hinge."

Maybe Alessio slammed doors once, but now he held the hard emotions inside. The worries, the anger—those emotions were buried under the princely cover. Happiness, joy, excitement—things that brought out smiles for others—seemed easier for him.

Brie had learned that in the little time she'd been with him. His brother, his king, knew it and was using it against him. Sebastian was dumping his own issues on the man who was doing his best for the country, for his brother.

"You shouldn't have said that." Brie's words were quiet as she stared at the closed door, willing Alessio to walk back through it.

Brie bit her lip, then turned her full attention to the king. "You shouldn't joke about him not having you in his life. My brother isn't in mine, and..." Her throat tightened as Beau's face danced in her mind. "You shouldn't wish for such things even if you don't want the crown."

Sebastian's eyes opened and color coated his cheeks. *Good.* He should think of his words and what they really meant.

She missed Beau. Their lives had separated. Or more accurately, their parents had separated them. It hurt to think that he'd not reached out to her. But he was still in their world.

Even if he'd never reached out for her, she'd never wish Beau gone. And if she found out he'd said it, she'd scream at him, demand he understood how much she needed him in the world, if not her life.

She opened the bag of muffins, mostly to give

herself something to do. The tops were perfect, and she wanted to chuck one at the king. "These are store-bought."

"No." Sebastian looked at her. "Homemade."

"Nope. They're from Lissa's Bakery downtown. Ophelia loves their orange ones. I always brought her one when she was having a bad week."

Brie lifted the muffin from the bag and showed the bottom of the confection, sugar and sweet wafting up from the pastry. "The little heart made with a C&D is her signature. It represents her children, Charlotte and Delia."

Sebastian cocked his head. "Quite the detective, Princess."

"Not a princess."

"Not yet."

He was trying to rile her up. She wasn't sure why, but Brie wasn't going to fall for it.

"Your brother loves you and he worries about you. You shouldn't toss that in his face."

"Even if he would be a better king?" Sebastian raised an eyebrow as he stood up from the couch. "The man that came back is exactly who father wanted on the throne. Ironic that it's him and not me."

"Especially for that reason. You grew up the heir." She held up her hand when he went to interrupt. "I'm not saying that was easy. I am sure it wasn't. But he grew up the spare, the replacement for you, a role no sibling should have to play."

When one thought about it, the ancient idea was quite sick.

"You are both more than the crowns on your heads. He is your brother. Don't let whatever personal issue made you lie about muffins get in between that."

"Careful, Princess." He took the muffin from her hand, taking a big bite out of it. He tilted his head, like he was trying to act brave or just redirect her focus. "You seem to be falling for him."

"I don't have to be falling for him to want to see him treated with care."

That was true. But it didn't change the fact that the words *falling for him* sent a wave of butterflies through her belly.

"If you say so." Sebastian took another bite of his muffin and wandered out of the media room. Brie looked at the marketing notes she had on the board. There was work to be done.

There is always work to be done.

Grabbing his forgotten coffee, and her own, she went in search of the man she most certainly wasn't falling for.

Alessio flipped and kept his body moving. The cool water slipping over him as he skimmed through the pool calmed him. At least it usually did. His fingers were wrinkling, but he didn't care as he flipped and pushed off the wall again. Move. Just move.

Usually twenty minutes was enough to burn off any unpleasant emotions. He wasn't sure how long he'd been gliding through the water, but the fury of his brother's words still wouldn't dissipate.

How could Sebastian have said such a thing? How could he have voiced such awful thoughts?

His brother was struggling with the crown, and Alessio was the reason for that. His argument— Alessio's rebellion. Even if Brie's scheme worked, it wasn't freedom he'd get. It wasn't freedom he deserved.

Sebastian needed him, even if he wouldn't say it directly. So the palace was where Alessio would stay.

Without Brie.

He pushed off the wall as sadness overtook him. Brie didn't deserve this gilded cage; he did. Losing his brother was not an option.

This is my place.

He shook his head in the water, wishing there was a way to wipe the pain of staying from his soul. He was his brother's helper. That was the way his father had always worded it.

Wanting to be more, his selfishness and his desire for freedom, had cost his family.

His shoulders burned as he reached the wall, but he didn't stop. He'd told the lifeguard to let him know when thirty minutes passed. It felt like that call should have come a while ago, but perhaps he was just tied up in his emotions.

That wasn't something he could let happen today. He and Brie had a full schedule, wedding dress shopping. It was an event she'd scheduled to cool the comments about them not wedding planning. It shouldn't be something he was looking forward to.

But part of him—the selfish part—wanted her with him. His partner in the life his choices forced on him.

He wanted to watch her walk down the aisle. He wanted to dance with her. Wanted to see her cut a chocolate wedding cake and eat lavender cookies. Wanted to see her smile. Wanted her beside him.

Brie made him laugh, she made him smile and she challenged him. She was fun to be around. With her he felt like the Alessio he'd once been. Not number two. Not the spare. Not the rebel that disappeared. With her he felt nothing more than a man. It was intoxicating.

Despite their unique situation, he felt like they were connected, meant to be.

Rationally he knew that was because they'd spent so much time together and because they were united in their quest for freedom.

But he wanted to believe she felt the connection, too.

Two legs appeared at the end of the lane, dangling in the water. She'd found him.

He didn't change the speed of his stroke, but his heartbeat picked up. He'd left Brie with his brother, an upset and pouty king. He'd wandered off and just left her.

Heat that had nothing to do with exercise flooded his cheeks. Sebastian had been in the mood for a fight, but Alessio had walked away, afraid that if he gave in, all the hurt he had would spill into the open. The wounds created as the spare had driven him from Celiana…and then had driven him back. But Sebastian didn't deserve the pain King Cedric had laid on Alessio.

But that wasn't an excuse for leaving Brie. What had he been thinking?

Lifting out of the water, he felt his mouth slip open at the sight of her holding out his coffee cup.

"You left this, and it was getting cold." She leaned over and dropped a kiss on his nose. "So I drank it."

"Heaven forbid we let coffee go to waste." Brie's bloodstream must be at least 50 percent caffeine.

"So glad you agree." She beamed as she reached around behind her back and pulled out a bottle of water. "This is probably more what you're looking for after a swim, though."

She uncapped it without asking, then passed it to him as she kicked her legs in the water.

The water tasted perfect. It was what his body craved. His soul—it craved her.

"Thank you. And I am sorry. I shouldn't have

left you with my brother. I was just…" His mind blanked on the right word.

"Angry. You were angry."

"He has a lot going on. The pressure of the crown. No one expected King Cedric's stroke. Despite being raised for it, I guess Sebastian thought he had more time before the weight of duty fell to him." The words slipped out, then he downed more of the water.

King Cedric's devotion was to Celiana. Everything else was second. It was that devotion Alessio tried to mimic with the Princess Lottery. It was that devotion that Sebastian continued to fail to meet.

Alessio was doing the best he could. But he wasn't the king.

Alessio swallowed and choked on the thoughts. He was number two. He'd always been number two.

"Sebastian does have a lot going on." Brie kicked her legs, water splashing up onto the T-shirt she wore. "But that doesn't mean you can't be angry about him joking about his demise. Or be angry that you have to step up. You are allowed to be angry."

Anger was emotion and emotions were normal, but if he gave in to them, he wasn't sure he'd stop.

"Sebastian expresses enough emotions for the both of us."

Leaning over, Brie cupped some water then

splashed it in his face. "Nope. One person does not get to express the emotions for another. Try again." The water splashed in his face, again, but this time he was ready.

"Brie, it's all right."

More water. "Seriously—"

More water.

"Say 'I was angry.'" She dumped more water on his head.

"I'm already wet!"

More water dropped on his head. It was coming quickly now.

"Fine. I was angry."

Brie beamed. "Why was that so hard?"

"I don't know." Except he did. He'd let his emotions rule once, and the consequences were catastrophic.

"Ugh. You're lying." Brie shook her head and let out a soft sigh. "If you don't want to tell me, just say it's not up for discussion. So much is not up for discussion with you anyway. I don't get it but...fine." She crossed her arms, tears hovering in her blue eyes. "See, anger. It's an emotion and you can give in to it."

He hated causing her tears and the acknowledgment that he was holding back. "I show emotions."

"The easy ones." Brie gripped the edge of the pool. "Joy, happiness or excitement. Fear, anger, hurt...those emotions are just as valid."

"I know." The words felt wrong on his tongue.

Since returning, he made sure no one saw his anger or his hurt.

How he'd yearned for something he could never have. He was a prince, born with a literal silver spoon in his mouth. How could he want more?

What kind of person did that make him?

Brie's brow furrowed, but she didn't call out the lie or splash him again.

"Do you need to swim more laps, work off the emotions I caused?"

There was no way to work off the feelings she brought out in him. In the two weeks she'd been at the palace, his world had shifted.

He'd expected that. You didn't get a lottery bride without everything changing, but he'd expected to still feel in control of himself.

He'd expected it would take time to know her, to be comfortable in her presence. Instead, his soul was dancing to a new and unknown rhythm.

"I killed my father." The words slipped into the open in the pool. They were words he'd never voiced, not even alone.

"No, you didn't." Brie slipped into the pool.

"You don't have on a swimsuit."

"Don't care." She wrapped her arms around him. "You didn't kill your father."

"I did, though." Alessio pinched his eyes closed. "King Cedric's plan for Sebastian's foreign bride fell through. So he dreamed up the Princess Lottery— for me. He was sure it would fix tourism. And he called me in Scotland, demanded I come home. Do the duty I'd refused for so long. I said…" His voice trailed off. He couldn't say the words. Couldn't give them voice.

"I said something I can't take back. Then he had his stroke. He never woke up. Never saw that I'd come home to do my duty."

"Alessio—"

"I am sorry that you got caught in the royal cage. Though with luck, you won't have to stay in it."

"We don't have to stay in it. You can still be whatever you want. Go back to Scotland."

There was a hesitation in her voice on the word *Scotland*. Or maybe he just hoped there was.

Sebastian needed him. He'd known that since before his brother's coronation. He'd seen it the first time everyone in the hospital room bowed to the new king as the old one was pronounced gone from the mortal plane. Alessio wasn't going anywhere. It was best to simply accept that.

"Enough about me. We have to get to Ophelia's. You're trying on wedding dresses and 'choosing' my suit."

Alessio made air quotes on the word *choosing*. He planned to enjoy the make-believe time. He might never see Brie in a wedding gown, but for today, today he could almost believe she'd be his.

"Nope." Brie kissed the tip of his nose, then swam away from him and started floating on her back.

"This morning was a lot, so I shifted the schedule. There are benefits to being best friends with the shop owner."

"What about the rumors? The articles. Do we need to take a photo of us in the pool? It will look sweet."

She floated over to him, her gaze locked on his. "What if today is just for us? And we don't think about the show part of it. We splash each other in the pool and have breakfast and watch a movie or take a walk where no one can see us. What if today we're just Alessio and Brie?"

Brie was so close to him, her eyes bright with an emotion he wanted to believe was hope that he'd say yes.

Like he'd ever say no to this.

"That sounds like heaven." It would be a little slice of perfection. Then he cupped a hand and splashed some water at her.

"You call that a splash?" She pushed an enormous wall of water toward him.

"Really, really, Princess. Is that how you want to play?"

Her giggle echoed behind another huge splash, and his heart exploded as she smiled at him.

Pulling her close, he was very aware of her body next to his.

"It's hard to splash you when you're holding me." Brie's cheeks were pink, but she didn't pull away from him.

"You want me to let go?"

"No." Brie captured his mouth.

Her fingers tangled in his wet hair, and he tightened his grip.

"Alessio."

His name on her sweet lips anchored him. Nothing mattered in this moment but her touch, her heat, her presence.

"Brie."

His fingers flirted with the edge of her wet shirt. He'd been her first kiss. They'd kissed so many times in the last fourteen days. It brought him joy each time.

But now, in this moment, his body ached to lift her from the pool, carry her to his rooms and forget everything else.

Her breasts pressed against him. She only had to say the words, and he'd do it. Lose himself in her.

She pulled back, desire blazing in her eyes, but the hint of hesitation was there, too. She pulled farther, and he didn't try to hold her. He wanted her desperately, but not before she was ready.

Alessio blew out a breath, then ran a thumb along her cheek. "Thank you for finding me."

"Anytime, Prince Charming."

She splashed more water, her laughter echoing around the pool, and he joined in the fun.

CHAPTER SEVEN

"PRINCESS! PRINCESS!"

It was weird to hear the title called out. The first time she'd heard it, Brie had nearly cried. Every other time, she'd used it as her focal point to make sure she kept her ideas on point. Today, though... today it felt different.

Her gaze flitted to Alessio, clearly getting into his role of dutiful heir to the throne. She understood now the reason the rebel returned the ever-dutiful heir to the throne. It was tragic.

But knowing it made her feel closer to the man beside her.

"Princess! Princess!" They were calling out for her. It should make her nervous. It always had before. That title symbolized the loss of everything she'd gained.

But it also meant Alessio. What if she could work and be a princess? What if the connection she'd believed was just the aftereffects of the lottery high was real? What if he was her match?

No. No. She wasn't traveling that path. This was a show. And they were getting far too good at the optics. That was all.

That didn't explain the pool or the meals they shared. No one was watching them then.

"So many people. I still have a hard time believing they're showing up."

"Everyone believes we're prepping for the wedding of the century, Brie. Trying on gowns—that's a can't-miss event. Our union is a big deal today. Tomorrow, we focus on some other tourist location." He held up his hands. "I know you sent me the schedule. I think it's an art gallery."

It was. And she knew he was playing with her. Alessio knew their schedule down to the minute.

"Right." It was the only word her tongue seemed capable of forming.

Our union.

Why had those words felt so right to hear, even when he was joking? This wasn't the life she'd planned for...the life she'd fought for.

If she turned her head, the flashing lights she could see in her periphery were all the reminder she needed. This life was the opposite of freedom.

Alessio would look delectable in a wedding suit. A wedding suit he'd wear when he pledged his heart to another.

Her heart raced and her stomach turned. He'd meet another at the altar, maybe in Scotland. Someone he chose, hopefully. And she'd be working in her downtown office, proving to her parents and everyone else that she didn't need them to accomplish her dreams.

Each was getting what they wanted...

There was no need for jealousy. This was a show. A role-play. A marketing campaign for the best Celiana offered. Nothing more.

Morning coffee...and kisses.

And why wasn't he saying anything! He was just staring at her, his deep green eyes holding hers.

Lifting a hand, he caressed her cheek. "You all right? You look as though you've seen a ghost."

Tiny bolts of electricity slipped along her skin. His mouth was so close to hers. They needed to pull apart, to get the show started. But she couldn't make herself move.

"Fine." Her voice quavered, and her breath seemed caught in her throat. "Just having a think on the agenda."

"Your brain is always spinning with ideas." He brushed his lips to hers.

The touch was so light, nothing like the passionate kisses they'd shared in the pool. Yet somehow it felt deeper.

The door to their car opened. She could hear the click of cameras, photographers capturing the perfect moment.

Except it hadn't been for the cameras. She saw the frown form on Alessio's face before he wiped it away. It was good they'd been caught in an organic kiss. But part of her wished the moment was just for them, too.

There is no us, Brie!

"Time to go, Prince Charming." She plastered on a smile as he leaned closer.

"You got this." Alessio's words were soft against her ear. Sweet and kind, but the worry wasn't for the crowd.

No. The crowd she could deal with. Her feelings for Alessio… She wasn't quite sure how to handle those.

"A kiss for the camera." Lev's voice was haughty and the first thing she heard upon exiting the car.

"We are engaged, Lev." Alessio smiled. It wasn't the full, beaming one that caused crinkles to show on the sides of his eyes, which was the smile that made her heart and soul dance when he showed it to her.

She squeezed his hand, then slid her arm around his waist. "Do you have an actual question?"

Lev's eyes lighted on hers. "You're supporting your best friend's shop. Do you plan to stay at your brother's new hotel for your honeymoon when it opens? Will any of Celiana's citizens not tied to you personally reap benefits from this—" Lev gestured to their joined hands "—union?"

Beau had a new hotel? So the rumor was true. It didn't surprise her. Their father had extolled the virtues of owning land, buildings and businesses at the dinner table. No time was spent on the children's days, other than admonishments if they'd fallen short of expectations. And they'd fallen short so often.

Still, she'd hoped that Beau would find his own way.

"I haven't spoken to my brother in years."

Each word felt like a tiny knife against her

tongue as she voiced publicly what she'd barely admitted in the privacy of her own home.

Alessio's hand tightened on her waist. Not much, just a touch tighter to remind her that she wasn't alone.

When they stopped this charade, she would be solo again. And the knife the question created cut even deeper.

"I wasn't aware that he was opening a hotel. As far as my dress goes, yes, Ophelia will design my wedding dress, but Alessio and I have plans for as many citizens as possible to participate in our wedding."

Our wedding.

She'd not actually meant to say that. In fact, Brie had carefully scripted her words to ensure she never actually said *wedding*. She hinted at it with marketing euphemisms designed to highlight where they were, not the nuptials they didn't plan to have.

"Will the press get that list?" Lev was calling her bluff.

"Of course." Alessio kissed the top of Brie's head. "I'll have it sent over this evening. Now, my fiancée and I have an appointment to get to."

Alessio nodded to the crowd, raising his hand to wave as they made their way to Ophelia's door.

"Why is the shop so dark?" Alessio's question echoed in the empty room. "Did Ophelia run off?"

"Without me?" Brie chuckled, though she was

as surprised as him to find the lights off and the blinds drawn. Usually the room was bright with natural light. "She better not have."

"I didn't," Ophelia called from the back. "I typically use natural light for these fittings. However, with all the camera flashes and such…" she offered as she came into the main room. "I've set up the back for you two. I told the press when they asked that the dress was a state secret."

Her friend beamed, clearly enjoying being in on the actual state secret.

Brie stepped into the back room and knew her mouth was hanging open. The storeroom was transformed. How much work had Ophelia put into this subterfuge?

The plan was to try on dresses and suits. That way they looked rumpled when leaving. Not disheveled but clearly tousled from trying on outfits. But the room looked like a real bridal setup.

Gauze hung over walls she knew were a dull gray. The boxes of materials usually stacked back here had vanished. The soft sofa she'd seen many brides' mothers sit on was back here, too.

She looked at the bright purple couch. The vibrant color popped against the gold gauze on the walls. Her mother would never sit there. No aunties would watch her try on dresses.

The walls seemed to close as she looked at the couch. What a silly thing to care about. Her mother hadn't been in her life in years. She'd not even reached out since Brie's name was drawn in the lottery. Maybe Lev asking about Beau had triggered the memories.

In her family's world, Brie no longer existed. If she crawled back, they'd take her. But the strong woman she was...that woman wasn't welcome. As she looked at the empty couch, the reality that this was just one more experience she'd lost hammered through her.

"Brie," Alessio and Ophelia spoke in unison.

Her eyes darted to her friend, then to Alessio. "My family isn't here."

He stepped to her side, pulling her into his arms, holding her. It felt perfect and it also reminded her of the illusion. Still, she couldn't step away.

"I'm sorry, Brie," Ophelia said. "The mothers, aunties, the family usually sit there. I didn't think when I pulled it back here."

"Why would you?" Brie let out a laugh that was far too close to a sob as Alessio stroked her back. "It's a couch. This shouldn't matter. It's just a couch."

His lips pressed into her forehead. "It represents what you've lost through no fault of your own. You are allowed to be upset by that. Even angry."

"Now anger is acceptable." Brie swallowed the lump in her throat.

"I thought you pointed out that it was always acceptable."

"Using my words against me, Prince Charming?"

"No." His lips brushed her forehead again as she looked up at him. "Just trying to help."

"Thank you." Stepping from his arms, Brie shook herself. "Well, that was quite the dramatic bridal moment!" She wiped a stray tear from her cheek. "But now we have a fashion show for the prince!"

"Yes." Ophelia looked from Brie to Alessio, a thought passing over her friend's face as she met her gaze.

Brie tilted her head, waiting for Ophelia to say whatever she was thinking.

Instead, she nodded to Alessio. "A fashion show for a prince. In my shop."

Brie smiled as Alessio sat on the couch and she followed her friend into the dressing area… She'd talked to Ophelia about finding her most outrageous dresses, the ones she'd designed because the idea just wouldn't leave her but she knew might never leave her racks.

Ophelia was an artist. Most of her designs were meant to sell, which meant they followed similar patterns: mermaid dresses, tight on the waist but flaring at the bottom, poufy princess ball gowns, sleek A-lines in shades meant for a bride.

But there were other dresses: over-the-top creations that fit on a runway or a magazine shoot. Those were dresses that Ophelia loved but doubted would ever sell. Brie had made Ophelia promise to pull as many of them as possible for this escapade.

The first dress did not disappoint. It was an actual mermaid theme, the blue bodice fading to sea green as it spilled past her feet.

"You are a dream in that gown. A mythical being. I swear, if your hair was wet, it would look like you just stepped out of the ocean."

Alessio grinned as she stood before him, but there was the hint of something in his eyes.

Disappointment.

She struck a pose, trying to bring out his real smile. The one she craved.

The dress hugged her in all the right places. It was beautiful, but there was no place for Brie to wear it. And it certainly wasn't a wedding dress.

And he'd expected to see one, expected to see her playing the part. She'd not counted on that. Her plans, her expectations for today, all vanished.

"Next one!" She dipped from the room and met Ophelia. "Can we put a few wedding dresses, like actual ones, in the rotation? Alessio—"

Brie cleared her throat as Ophelia raised a brow. "Like a dress you might wear down the aisle?"

"I mean, I'm not walking down the aisle, but he…" Again her throat closed as she looked at the closed door of the dressing room.

She could picture Alessio sitting on the couch. Picture him waiting, hoping that she'd step out in a wedding dress, even for a fashion show he knew was fake.

The fact that she wasn't, the look on his face, the acceptance hiding hurt…

"I set aside a few earlier. I'll grab them."

Brie nodded, ready for the next few hours of dress-up.

After an hour of trying on dresses, playing princess, Brie couldn't take her eyes off herself. The image in the mirror *was* a princess, a woman she could see walking toward Alessio.

The soft gold glimmered on her skin. The scalloped bodice hugged her breasts as the A-line dress slipped over her hips. The simple cut contrasted with the delicate flowers embroidered from the bodice to the train. They were the flowers of Celiana.

This dress…

His mouth would fall open. He'd smile, a real one, dimples, creases around his eyes. He'd beam as she walked toward him.

It was easy to imagine. Easy to see.

"I can't show him this one." The whispered words hung in the dressing room.

Ophelia wrapped her arms around Brie. "I've seen this moment many times before with my brides."

"This moment?" Brie placed her hands on her stomach, staring at the image in the mirror.

"When they find the one. This is your wedding dress."

Except she didn't need a dress. Even one as perfect as this, which she could see herself wearing while standing next to him. His hands were reaching for her over the altar as they promised forever.

"I'm not marrying Alessio. I'm not." The words were soft, barely audible. Brie wasn't even sure she'd managed to push them out.

"Who are you trying to convince? Me? Or yourself?" Ophelia squeezed her shoulders.

"I have my company."

"Maybe you could have both…" Ophelia met her gaze in the mirror.

"Princesses don't have careers." Brie hiccuped as she looked at the gown. "This isn't my gown. It's beautiful, but it isn't mine."

"Brie—"

"This isn't real. I'm not the protagonist in a fairy tale. Alessio and I have a deal and a goal to *not* meet at the altar. We aren't in love."

Aren't in love. Why did saying that out loud hurt so much? It was a marketing scheme—her best plan ever. But it wasn't real.

Apparently her heart would need her brain to remind her of that more often.

"Honey." Ophelia's gaze was full of questions Brie didn't want to answer.

"Time for Alessio to try on suits. My turn on the couch." The words were rushed, and her emotions were spilling everywhere as she looked at the gown in the mirror one last time.

This was a dream.

Alessio and she got on well. He was sweet, and he was kind. And his kisses awoke places in her body…

In another time, another place, maybe they'd have found each other. Found happiness.

But that wasn't this time. It wasn't this place. And her heart felt like it was cracking as Ophelia helped her out of the wedding dress.

"You look like you stepped from a fairy tale." Brie clapped as Alessio stepped from the dressing room.

"You've said that about the last three suits." Alessio playfully crossed his arms. "I know there isn't as much difference in these as your dresses, but still…"

Brie laughed and he moved toward her, dropping a kiss on her lips. "Do you like this one more or less than the last two?"

"Can I be honest?"

His heart pounded against his ribs as he looked at her. She'd not shown him the last dress. He didn't know why. She'd said that it hadn't fit right. A lie, he suspected, but something had shifted.

She was laughing at all the right moments, clapping and having a good time—she'd even posted a picture of him in the first suit and asked people to weigh in—but there was a look in her eye, like she was assessing him each time he walked out. It was like she was actually looking for a suit.

Of course she wasn't. And he shouldn't want her to. Though that didn't stop the rebel from wishing that maybe she was thinking of staying no matter what the marketing scheme produced.

He tried pushing those selfish thoughts away.

"So what is your honest feeling on these suits, Briella?"

"That you looked delectable in each of them, but they are very similar. Each of my dresses was different. The mermaid gown to the last…"

The last.

She'd hesitated. What was the last dress, the one she'd refused to show him?

Brie looked away, so he focused on the other part of her sentence.

"Delectable?"

Her cheeks darkened but she met his gaze, desire burning in his eyes. "You know you're attractive, Prince Charming." She shook a finger at him playfully. "Searching out compliments? Really?"

He knew he was conventionally attractive, that he met society's definition of handsome.

It wasn't society's definition he wanted, though.

"It's still nice to hear." He kissed her again. Since opening up in the pool, they'd kissed so freely. It was a gift he didn't deserve, but he couldn't stop worshipping her lips. "Ophelia has one more option. Though it sounds like you could pick any of these options and be happy with the outcome."

"Alessio—"

He captured her lips before she could argue that there was no need to pick out wedding attire. He knew that. It was a slip of the tongue, a wishful thought. But he didn't want the reminder right now.

"Go!" Brie pushed at his shoulders after he broke the connection. "Maybe the next suit will be magic."

He stood and headed back to the dressing area. The suit he'd seen on the rack was gone. Alessio looked in the dressing room. Nothing.

"Ophelia?"

She rounded the corner, a dress bag slung over her arm. "I don't think the final suit I picked before is a good fit."

"Oh." Alessio didn't quite know how to respond. He didn't think of his clothes that much. It was a statement of privilege, he knew, as was the fact that he had a personal shopper who knew his tastes and the clothes appeared when he needed them.

His mother thought more about her outfits. He'd heard her argue that people were going to talk about what she wore, how she wore it and when she wore it, so she might as well make the statement she wanted with the clothes on her body.

"The suits seem fine." He pulled a hand over his face. Those were not the words to give a designer, but what else was there to say?

"*Fine* is not what we are going for." Ophelia sucked in a breath, then looked at the closed door. He knew she was seeing beyond it to the woman on the other side.

The best friend she'd offered aid to flee the island.

"*Fine* is not what one wears to a royal wedding, Your Royal Highness."

He shook his head. "Ophelia?" She knew this wasn't real. Knew they were here only because the hints of rumors were bothering Brie. Hell, the only reason they were trying on outfits was because Brie was worried if they came out looking too perfect, people might suspect they'd only sat and chatted with Ophelia.

That was a worry that would never have crossed his mind. Her brain saw all the patterns, the questions people might ask, like his saw the potential in glass.

"Just humor me." Ophelia pushed past him into the dressing room and hung the bag on the wall hanger.

Alessio waited in the hall, not wanting to crowd the woman. Brie's family was gone—not from the mortal world, but from her life. Ophelia was her sister, not by blood, but in all the ways that mattered.

Ophelia nodded as she stepped from the room. "If you can give her choices, then maybe there will be a royal wedding."

Choices.

The word hung in the silent hallway. Choices were not what royals got. The country came first. What royals wanted came in a distant second.

Brie deserved more than that. Still, Ophelia's words hung in his soul.

Brie deserved all the choices. He could give her that, behind the palace's closed walls. In public, they'd be supporters of his brother, beholden to the people of Celiana. In the palace… His brain ceased the conversation as his heart screamed that it wasn't enough.

But what if it was?

Rather than try to voice anything, Alessio stepped into the room and quickly donned the suit.

It was a charcoal gray, with a gold tie. The cut was similar to the other suits, highlighting his broad shoulders and slim waist.

It wasn't all that different from the black and navy suits Ophelia had shown him, but it felt right. That was a weird feeling for a suit.

He stepped into the hallway, and Ophelia raised a hand, covering her mouth.

"I take it you think this is the one, too." Alessio chuckled and reached for the door handle. "Shall we see what my Brie thinks?"

He stepped into the room and saw Brie's mouth open, then shut. Her eyes flicked behind him. He wasn't sure what the silent communication was, but he didn't stop looking at her.

"What do we think of gray and gold?"

"Perfect." Brie pursed her lips, tilted her head, took a step toward him, then stopped. "It's a perfect wedding look."

"Brie?" He closed the distance between them. She looked happy, but also terrified. Two emotions he'd never seen together. "What's wrong?"

"Nothing." She shook her head against his

shoulder. "Nothing is wrong. Why is nothing wrong?" Her nervous laugh echoed in the back room.

He looked to Ophelia and then back, unsure what to say. "You want something to be wrong?"

"We're picking out wedding outfits."

"Not really." He pressed a kiss to the top of her head. "We're playing dress-up." That was such a bitter truth.

"We're weeks into this charade."

Charade.

His soul rioted against that word. It was a charade. And he hated that. This wasn't what she'd planned, but they were having fun together.

Her kisses were not what he should be focusing on in this moment.

"We're picking out a gown and a suit and it should feel *wrong*. This isn't supposed to make me—"

Her words cut off and Ophelia's words echoed in his mind. *If you can give her choices...* Could he keep her? Could he actually have her as a partner in the life he hadn't wanted? Would she stay?

"Brie." He pulled her into his arms, unsure what to say but needing her with him. Her body relaxed into his. He rested his head on hers, soaking in the moment.

CHAPTER EIGHT

"Brie!"

"Briella!"

"Princess!"

Calls echoed from around the market stalls. Everyone wanted to see Celiana's future princess.

Brie was doing great. She'd waved when they'd exited the vehicle. Then she'd answered a few questions and taken so many floral offerings he suspected their vehicle would smell of pollen, sweetness and leaves on the way back to the palace.

People were snapping photos, and he'd heard more than one person mention how they'd never have thought to come to the markets if Brie wasn't here.

She was a hit. And her idea was working. What would happen when she left? Would the excitement continue without her?

And would he be able to keep going?

Of course he would. He had to. Still, Alessio knew it would be fake smiles greeting the people then—even if they never realized it.

"Prince Alessio." Lev's voice echoed behind him. The royal tabloid reporter, despite his claims of hating everything about this "spectacle," was at each event.

His father had taken the position of answering Lev's questions in the past, granting him access like all other journalists. Sebastian had questioned the policy but left it in place.

Lev hated the royal family, even though they were the reason people clicked on his opinion pieces, the reason he made as much money as he did. Whether his antagonism was for website clicks or a true dislike, Alessio didn't know. Nor did it matter.

The man was going to write the articles he wanted; at least this way the palace got a little control.

"How does it feel to be third now?" Lev looked over Alessio's shoulder, clearly watching Brie with the crowd. "Always second fiddle to someone, huh?"

Second fiddle.

He felt his jaw twitch and he saw the gleam in Lev's eyes.

Second fiddle. Spare. Extra. Those were words his father used constantly. And they were words Alessio hated, words he never heard when he'd left.

"Briella is doing a lovely job. I'm proud that my fiancée is so loved by the people." The bite of jealousy in his heart had nothing to do with Brie.

She was a natural. But a lifetime of second fiddle, a lifetime of hearing the phrase, from those he loved and those he very much did not, still stung.

"People think this is more of a marketing stunt than a love story. Any comment?"

Alessio tilted his head and wanted to curse. Reacting to such a statement was a tell, one he was usually very good at controlling.

Technically, everything the palace did was a

marketing stunt. They used their image for power, but Brie was elevating the game.

"I don't really think that needs a comment." Alessio smiled at a small boy who handed him a picture of him and Brie.

"What about people who say that Sebastian should be the one doing this? That you're stealing your brother's spotlight? The spare rising above his position."

"*King* Sebastian." Alessio emphasized the title the reporter had omitted, enjoying the hint of color invading Lev's cheeks. It was one thing to disparage the royals at the keyboard, another to do it to their faces.

"King Sebastian is busy taking over from King Cedric. He didn't plan to take the crown so suddenly." So suddenly. The stroke, brought on by Alessio's argument. Or at least elevated by it. No matter what Brie thought.

Sebastian seemed to wilt as the crown he'd been raised to wear landed on his head. Alessio wasn't sure what had happened, and the few times he'd brought it up, Sebastian had changed the subject or just walked away.

Sebastian was the one their father loved, the one he'd doted on. Of course his grief would take a different course from Alessio's.

So he'd done what he hadn't before. He'd stepped into his duties. It was as simple—and complicated—as that.

"You didn't answer my question." Lev raised a brow.

"What question?" Brie's sweet voice was tinged with fire, though he doubted Lev realized it, as she slipped her fingers into his. "What question?" she repeated as she looked from Lev to Alessio.

"I asked if he had any comment on people saying that Alessio was overshadowing *King* Sebastian."

"Are people saying that or are you typing it and hoping they'll agree?" Brie's voice was steady as she squeezed Alessio's hand. Then she pointed to a stall. "I want to see that."

She pulled Alessio away without waiting for Lev to comment. He looked over his shoulder, unsurprised to see Lev make a note on his phone.

"He's going to stir that into some kind of rumor." Alessio made sure his words were only for her ears. To others it would look like he was whispering sweet nothings.

"Probably." Brie's bright blue eyes held his. "But we'll deal with it."

We. He loved that word when it was applied to them.

Brie leaned her head against his shoulder as they made their way through the crowded area, the security team a few feet behind and in front of them.

He kissed the top of her head; he loved touching her, getting close to her. The motions weren't for the cameras he knew were everywhere, not anymore.

"Brie!"

"Brie!"

"You're quite popular, my dear." He let the endearment run off his lips.

Brie's cheeks tinted pink, and he put his hand around her waist. "Popularity is easy. Keeping their focus on the important things is harder."

She kissed his cheek, then pulled him toward the stalls. "Come on."

"Of course." Brie was right. Today was supposed to be about highlighting the stalls, not them.

She leaned over a stall with a few handmade bags he was sure she'd pointed to randomly when she dismissed Lev. "These are lovely."

"Thank you, Princess. I'm glad I came this weekend. I almost didn't with prices for travel—" The seller cut off her words. "Anyway…"

"You've struggled?" Brie's voice was even, and Alessio looked over a few bags in the stall to give them at least the appearance of privacy.

"Who hasn't?" The woman sighed. "I mean, I guess you—"

"My parents disowned me a few years ago. I spent days living off coffee and stress as rent came due. My upbringing was very privileged—I can't deny that—but I've also known what it feels like to be terrified that I'd lose my tiny studio apartment."

The woman reached over and gripped Brie's hand. "My parents passed two years ago. I've taken over the care of my teen sister. I started making bags to sell to supplement the income as tourist visits dipped at our family restaurant.

"But since the lottery," the woman continued, her tone instantly brightening, "it's been quite full. I don't need to be here, but these—" She looked at the bags. "My mother always called it a hobby. But it…"

"It makes you feel whole." Brie grinned.

She really was in her element here. Alessio saw the young woman relax, Brie's calming presence giving her something he couldn't describe. If she stayed, married him, she'd be such an asset to the royal family.

And that was exactly why she should leave.

No one should be an asset.

"They're just bags." The woman bit her lip as she looked over her wares.

"No." Brie picked up a small white leather bag that looked big enough to carry a cell phone and maybe a tube of lipstick. It wasn't practical, but Alessio could see the craftsmanship.

"That's part of my bridal collection—guess you're drawn to it."

"I guess I am." Brie grinned. "I'll take it."

"Oh. No, it's my gift to you, Princess."

Brie shook her head. "I appreciate the kindness,

but lesson one in business—don't turn away paying customers. Even if they wear a crown."

She laughed, then looked to Alessio. "Except, who has our money?" Her cheeks darkened as she looked from the purse to the woman behind the small counter.

By rule, the royal family didn't carry wallets or cash on them. People sent their bills to the palace. Or they did just as the woman suggested and offered things as a gift.

Alessio handed the woman a card. "Send the bill here, and the palace will make sure you're compensated."

"Thank you."

"And I'll check," Brie added. "Send the bill!"

"Yes, Princess."

Alessio wrapped an arm around her waist as they left the stall. "You are amazing. Just so you know."

Brie hit his hip with hers. "I am. But the reason her hobby has a chance to become a business is because her restaurant is thriving again."

He heard the hesitation in her voice. "The lottery did what I intended. Your marketing…" He paused, barely catching himself before the word *scheme*. Her marketing was more than a scheme, and there were ears and cameras all around. "It's working."

"If we don't meet at the altar…" The whispered words vanished into the commotion of the crowd.

But he didn't need to hear the end of the sentence. If they didn't meet at the altar, would the kingdom continue to thrive? Brie's plan was brilliant. It should have been instituted years ago. But was it sustainable without the wedding? He wasn't sure. When they separated, shattered the illusion, would the kingdom suffer?

All were questions to consider, but his brain was focusing on one word. *If.*

If we don't meet.

Not when. It shouldn't bring him so much pleasure, but damn. His heart felt like it wanted to jump out of his chest.

"Oh!" Brie brightened as a glasswork stall came into view. The light struck the handblown glass; it was a sight to see.

"Did you make this?" Brie stepped into the stall, her mouth hanging open as she looked at the art on the shelves.

The man's weathered hands had held the tools for molding liquid glass into the most beautiful pieces for over forty years. Emilio taught a class at the college Alessio had attended. And Alessio had been fascinated from the moment he'd shaped his first piece.

He'd learned everything possible from the master glassworker.

"Emilio is the island's only master glassblower." Alessio looked over the art, amazed, as always, at his friend's ability. The glass pieces molded in his tools, whether dinnerware cups or ornamental works, were masterpieces.

"Not true. You are here, too." Emilio stepped from the booth and reached for Alessio's hand. "What have you made recently?"

It was his standard question. Not *How are you?* or *What's new?* but *What have you made?*

"I've been a bit busy."

"You said you were a glassworker but…" Brie's eyes were bright as she looked at Emilio's art. "You blow glass? Like this?"

"Not anymore." Alessio bit the inside of his cheek, fighting the urge to ask Emilio if he'd seen the recent exhibit in Paris. The images Alessio had looked at on his computer made his hands itch to craft something. But he'd put that world behind him.

"Alessio?" Her voice pulled him back.

"Let me introduce you to my fiancée, Brie Ailiono." He smiled, ignoring the questions he didn't want to answer in Brie's eyes.

Emilio reached for her hand, but Alessio saw more than a hint of reservation in his eyes.

"I was at your family estate last week," Emilio said to Brie.

Brie's body shifted as she leaned toward Alessio—reaching for him, seeking him.

"I'm not in contact with my family."

"They said as much." Emilio pursed his lips, then clicked his tongue.

Alessio knew he was weighing his words. He'd heard the click so many times in the man's workshop. It was a tell Emilio knew about but was unable to stop. Except there wasn't a piece of artwork needing critique.

"Emilio—" Alessio wrapped his arm around Brie's waist. If his friend had heard something important, they needed to know. The Ailiono family was powerful; anyone who doubted that found out at their peril.

"What am I missing?" Brie's gaze met his.

"Emilio clicked his tongue. I was his student for years. It means he's weighing a tough set of words." Alessio squeezed her. "What aren't you saying, Emilio?"

"Your family hired me for a big piece of art. In your old room. Told me to throw everything out. Not what I was paid for, but some clients..." He cleared his throat.

Some clients were entitled. Alessio had run into more than one during the three years he'd run his own shop. One client screamed that the art he'd commissioned was too big. When Alessio reminded him that it was the exact measurements he'd requested, the man had become apoplectic.

"I'm surprised my stuff was even still there." Brie smiled but her eyes didn't light up. The bouncy spirit she'd had with the woman in the previous stall was absent.

"They said marrying the prince in a lottery was beneath an Ailiono." Emilio's words were direct.

Beneath an Ailiono. Only that family would think having a royal bride was beneath them. Sure, the lottery was different, but it wasn't like the Ailionos' unions weren't also arranged. That was why Brie had fled.

"Your mother said that if you followed through with it, there was no hope for you."

Brie's breath hitched but she didn't say anything. Was she mourning that loss or realizing a door she thought closed forever had a crack? At least it had, until her name rose from the lottery drawing.

Until this moment, Alessio had never understood the phrase *I saw red*. The color danced across his eyes. He was mad at the Ailionos, mad at Emilio, mad at the situation as a whole.

"Emilio—" His voice was harder than intended. It was the tone he used as Prince Alessio in the rare cases where a strong royal persona was necessary. Brie wrapped an arm around him, squeezing his side just like he'd done for her.

Emilio held up a hand. "I do not say this to hurt you, but I wanted to explain why—" he looked over his shoulder "—why I brought something to the market this weekend."

He turned and went behind the bench that served as his checkout stand. "Your campaign to showcase the island makes it easy to know where you'll be."

Campaign.

He saw Brie shift. The rumors were still there, not as squashed as she'd hoped. But that was a worry for another day.

Emilio pulled out a box overflowing with pictures and trinkets. "I managed..." He cleared his throat. "I'm sure I didn't get everything important to you, Princess, but these things looked loved."

Brie took one step toward the box, paused, then quickly closed the distance.

Her fingers reached for the box, her shoulders shaking as she looked over the trinkets of her girlhood. She'd mentioned leaving, but this box meant she'd truly fled. She'd left behind nearly everything.

She lifted pictures, holding them up to show him. Some people in the images he recognized, while others were acquaintances that moved in similar circles. She flipped through a few notebooks and journals, laughing to herself.

"These were my secret dream journals. I had to hide them under my bed."

Emilio nodded.

And her parents were throwing everything out, all the things she might have cherished.

Brie ran a hand over one of the journals. Her face was so full of excitement over a secret dream journal.

It was a secret because she couldn't be Brie. Until she'd left their home, she'd been Briella, the daughter of the wealthiest man in the nation, but not a loved child. She'd been an object for gain. It was only when she left that she became herself.

Freedom.

Worry pressed against his chest. He didn't want to steal that from her. But he also didn't want to give her up. If he gave her choices, perhaps he could find a way to make her want to stay.

Brie was so much more than a pretend lottery bride. She was the woman who listened to his darkest secret, comforted him, then splashed him with water. She was the woman who could take a simple outing and turn it into a viral marketing campaign. She was the one he was falling for. Truly falling for.

A small bumblebee stuffie rose and she let out a sob. Alessio pulled her to him without thinking. If she was upset, then her place was in his arms.

"My brother gave this to me when I was five or six. He used to joke that I was always buzzing around him. When I left, I was so alone, no one to bother. I always wondered if Beau missed me. Or if he was grateful the annoying sister was finally gone."

He kissed the top of her head, holding her tightly, reminding her that she wasn't alone. Not as long as she was with him.

He held her for several minutes, letting her gather herself.

Finally, Brie pulled back and walked around the bench, pulling Emilio into her arms. "Thank you. Thank you so much."

"Consider it an early wedding present." Emilio hugged her.

"No one will be able to top it, Emilio." Alessio winked. This was a gift Brie would remember for forever.

Brie stepped back and wiped a tear from her cheek.

"Make me a promise, Princess." Emilio tilted his head as he looked at Alessio. "Make him show you his studio. Don't let him give up his gift."

"I plan to see it. As soon as we return to the palace." Brie nodded, determination clear in her features.

"Wow!"

Brie couldn't believe the "small" studio she was standing in was Alessio's glassworks studio. It was organized chaos. Designs covered the walls, sketches that were gorgeous on their own but that he could craft in glass in their image. The man was a master.

"Alessio." She whispered his name as she walked past the drawings and then saw a completed piece on the table. Twisted flames licked up at an indistinguishable human figure. Whether the man was beating the flames or consumed by them was up for interpretation.

"That was the second-to-last piece I created." His eyes hovered on the piece, a frown hinting at the edge of his lips. "I haven't been in the shop as much this year."

Consumed by the flames.

He'd put all his efforts into saving Celiana through the bride lottery. And it was working. She'd heard that throughout the market stalls today.

People were seeing improvements. They were smiling and happy to have the prince and future princess in their places. And just like in Ophelia's shop last week, it felt natural. It felt like where she was supposed to be.

It's because I've been doing it for over a month. I've been living and breathing this life. That's all.

And maybe fear. She'd lost nearly all the jobs she'd lined up during the bride lottery. No matter what line she gave, no matter the hints she dropped, they all assumed when she wed that the princess wouldn't work. And she couldn't come right out and say she was planning to leave Alessio. Not yet.

The idea of walking away from him, from the man that understood her need for freedom, understood the craving, grew more painful with the passing days. This was a fake relationship; it was. And it was impacting the company she'd built.

If she didn't have her business…what did she have?

Alessio. She had Alessio. If she wanted him. If she was willing to step into this life, hold his hand and walk this path.

So many ifs…and yet none of them felt insurmountable. They felt…they felt perfect. And that was terrifying.

They could continue as they were, marketing Celiana. It was different and not a traditional job. There'd be no penthouse suite…but the success might be more meaningful.

He was grinning as he walked to his furnace, his hands running along pipe-looking fixtures next to it. This was his happy place. This was the place the real Alessio loved most.

The pool was where he worked off unsettled emotions. This…this was his sanctuary.

"You should have seen my shop in Scotland. It was this tiny cottage. I sold my wares in the front and the back was my workshop."

"Scotland. You had a shop there?"

Alessio turned, his face lit with happiness. "It was the best place. Mine. I was a glassworker. No one even knew I was a prince of Celiana. Three years I got to take orders and live as a creative."

"You could do it again."

Alessio shook his head. "No. My place is by Sebastian. I might get to play in here more—after all your plan is working. But my own shop full-time—that dream is over."

He reached for her hand, squeezing it before stepping away. "The glass ball everyone put their lottery tickets in was my last major piece. I knew that when I made it."

"You made that?" It had been large, so large. She took her phone from her back pocket and pulled up her social media page. She scrolled back and found an image she'd taken in front of the entry post.

The large ball was on spinners. She'd joked on more than one occasion that the intricate hearts traced in the ball were over-the-top, but she'd privately admitted that ball was lovely. On sunny days, rainbows formed in the glass. Press releases had talked about how it was a sign of good fortune.

And she'd have never guessed that it was sculpted by Prince Alessio.

"Why didn't you tell everyone? That is a story the press would have eaten up!" The marketeer in her wanted to scream at the lost opportunity. The stories she'd have spun in Ophelia's dresses...

Plus, it added depth to Alessio. It let the world see the man she saw.

"Because." He wrapped her in his arms. Time froze as his green eyes held hers. The urge to tickle him, to make him laugh, nearly overwhelmed her, but she wanted to hear his answer. "Then they would have wanted to see my workshop. There'd be pressure to film me creating something."

"True."

Everyone would want to see it. Would that be so bad? Prince Alessio had a secret creative side. The dutiful prince was so much more than just the image he projected. More than the interviews projected, more than the crown. More than the reformed rebel.

Alessio was funny, kind, silly. He was a full person, but the rest of the country didn't get to see that man. Why?

"Heaven forbid that the world should learn that you are a master glassworker."

Her fingers brushed along his jaw, enjoying the feel of his beard.

Alessio leaned his head against hers. "This is mine. I didn't want to share it. But if you want to post about it, I can strike a pose."

It would be the perfect story. But she knew she'd never post a single image in here. As long as he wanted this to be only his, that was how it would stay. He'd given so much up for Celiana already; she could give him this space.

"It can be our little secret, Alessio."

He kissed the top of her head. "Want to make something?"

"Make something? How would I even do that?"

Alessio pulled back and pushed a few buttons on the wall. The furnace made a few loud noises that must be normal since he didn't blink an eye at them, then it kicked to life.

"I taught classes in Scotland on the side. Taught others the craft. My shop was the one place in the world I was number one."

Brie's heart turned on his words. "Alessio."

He held up a hand. "I didn't mean anything bad, Brie. Want to give it a go?"

She was torn. She wanted to see him in this place, witness the true artist emerge. But she wanted to touch the hurt spot in his heart, too. That was the place that claimed he was only the spare, the man caring for the new king, the one who felt responsible for his father's demise.

He was so much more.

"Yes."

He flipped a few more switches and grabbed supplies from around the shop. She watched his face relax and the stiffness leave his shoulders. She watched him come into himself. His face was open, free of duty.

"All right, come here."

She moved to the furnace, letting him guide her. He handed her safety goggles, then directed her behind a small metal-and-wood table beside the furnace. His hands were firm on her hips as he shifted her slightly.

"Relax, Brie."

That might be possible if his hands weren't resting on her hips.

"Trying."

Alessio grabbed a blowpipe and fitted it against the hole in the furnace before coming back with the molten glass.

"Whoa." It was one thing to know he did this

with such skill, another to see the red-orange glass.

"I got you." He placed the pipe on the table, the glass hanging off, and wrapped her hands around the pipe. Then he stepped behind her again, pressing his body against hers.

He whispered instructions in her ears. Brie did her best to follow them, but all her mind could think of was the man behind her, the feel of him against her, the promise of what might be.

Her life had changed, altered completely. The idea of leaving, escaping, no longer felt like an absolute necessity. If she was honest, the thought of leaving hurt.

Together they molded the glass, turned it, twisted it, made it into something new.

That was what this relationship was. Her heart rate pulsed in her ears; she felt her face flush and it had nothing to do with the heat of the room. It was him, the man whose body made her sing with promises she'd never sought.

The man she was falling for.

Her brain had tried to ignore the attachment. "See?"

She blew out a breath. As she looked at the molten blob he'd pulled from the furnace, it transformed into a heart. It was weird how one second it was nothing, but now it was something.

Just like us.

They were something now.

But what did that mean for the future? Brie wasn't sure, but for tonight, she wanted to pretend they weren't the prince and his lotto bride. Just Brie and Alessio.

"Ta-da!" Alessio's lips skimmed her neck before he took the pipe from her hands. It was a glass heart with a yellow one inside. Beautiful.

"Nice work, Brie." He dropped a kiss on her cheek before taking the heart to a little box in the corner. "Needs to cool."

"Alessio—" she walked toward him "—I did very little of that. It was all you."

"It was us." His eyes glittered.

She couldn't stop herself from moving. She wrapped her arms around him, capturing his lips. Tomorrow she'd start to figure out the conflict between what her heart felt and her mind wanted. Tonight, all she needed was the man before her.

Need, desperate to make him hers, completely wrapped through her.

"Take me to bed, Alessio."

Take me to bed.

Alessio lifted Brie in his arms, the weight of her body a thrill on his already warm skin. Standing behind her, holding her hands as they molded the glass, had been as blissful as Alessio ever thought to get. But her words and her lips, they dragged him even further toward heaven.

Her lips pressed against his neck, her fingers

ran along his chest, and it took every ounce of attention to ignore the flames licking at him to ensure they made it to his bedroom as smoothly as possible.

Brie laughed as he kicked open the door. "I swear that is a movie move, Alessio."

"Maybe." His mouth lowered, drinking her in, savoring the moment.

He laid her on the bed and her hands immediately flattened, her face changing.

"Brie..." Her whispered name burned on his lips. "If you've changed your mind—"

"No, but—" she pursed her lips and he saw her swallow "—what if I'm bad at this?"

"Not possible." Alessio lifted her fingers, placing a soft kiss against each one before dropping her hand. "Tonight is yours, Briella." He opened his arms and saw his words register.

"Just like my first kiss." Brie sat up on her knees, her hands threading under his shirt.

This would be the most blissful torture. But Alessio would not deny her the moment.

Her hands explored him. She lifted his shirt over his head, a smile radiating across her lips. "You are so magnificent."

Alessio's fingers found the edge of her top and his body quivered as she raised her hands. Her red lace bra nearly brought him to his knees.

"You are the magnificent one, Brie."

His lips trailed along her collarbone, and she reached behind herself to unhook her bra.

They explored each other, and he made a mental note at every breath change, every sigh. Bringing her pleasure and driving her to wonder were the only thoughts in his brain.

When she lay beneath him, Alessio dragged his lips across her thighs before finding her inner core. Brie bucked under his dancing mouth as he devoured her. She was sweet and fire and everything he needed.

"Alessio!"

Her cry as he felt her body tighten turned him on even more. He'd not thought it possible. He stroked her with his fingers, bringing her to bliss again. Then he pulled the condom down his length.

The urge to drive himself to the hilt pulsed against every nerve, but he held himself steady as he pressed into her folds.

Brie wrapped her legs around him, pulling him deeper. She took a long breath.

"You are so beautiful," Alessio whispered against her ear, holding himself steady until she started moving against him.

They found their rhythm and he lost all thoughts of anything besides the woman with him. This was as close to heaven as he'd ever get and he was savoring every moment.

CHAPTER NINE

BLOND HAIR SPILLED over his chest, and Alessio gently stroked Brie's back. The urge to touch her, to convince himself that she was here, that he'd spent last night worshipping her body and was not trapped in one of his dreams, cruised through him.

He'd once heard a friend say the afterglow of being with his girlfriend, now wife, was the best feeling in the world. It was how he knew he wanted to propose, to ensure he spent the rest of his life with a person who made him feel so whole.

Alessio, like many of the guys in attendance, had laughed. The stereotype that women enjoyed snuggling, but men moved on, ran deep in their youthful subconscious.

Now though, as he held Brie in the early hours, he knew what his friend had meant. He knew how deep the feeling was, and the rightness of being exactly where you belonged.

But what did belonging to a prince mean for her?

"What time is it?" Brie mumbled as she lifted her head. The hair spilled over her eyes, and her lips were luscious and calling to be kissed.

"Just after six. I found a way to keep you in bed." He grinned, then brushed his lips over hers. "How are you this morning?"

He'd been gentle and made sure she reached the heights of making love, but that didn't shift that last night had been her first time. Mentally, and physically, that was a big deal. And it was the only reason he hadn't woken her this morning with kisses trailing along her magnificent body.

"Deliriously happy." Her fingers danced along his chest. Pink rose in her cheeks and her smile radiated straight to his heart.

"Deliriously happy." He kissed the tip of her nose, unable to keep from kissing her. "I love the sound of that."

He loved her.

The words hovered in the back of his mind. It hadn't been intentional, and suddenly all the things she'd have to give up by his side hit even harder. But her marketing plan was working. She could get her freedom…and what would that mean for his heart?

"We need to get breakfast." Brie rolled over and sighed.

"And you want coffee," Alessio teased.

"How well you know me." Brie laughed. "I'm going to head to my room. I'll see you soon." She dropped a kiss to his lips, then slid from the bed, grabbed her clothes and headed through the connecting door to her room.

It was the first time she'd used it, and he couldn't describe the burst of happiness that floated through him to see it open now.

Alessio rose from the bed and grabbed his phone. The text from his assistant, Jack, made him smile. They had a state function tonight. It would be his brother's first; he was welcoming a foreign dignitary from Europe. The staff had worked hard on the function, but it wasn't his concern.

Brie and Alessio were attending as ornamentation only. The spare and his future bride, they'd have the night mostly to themselves while everyone was focused on King Sebastian's first state dinner. But he had a surprise for her. And it had been delivered this morning.

He quickly donned some slacks and a comfortable shirt and went in search of Brie.

She was sitting on the bed, and he saw a tear slip down her cheek.

"Brie?" He moved to her side, sitting beside her and pulling her to him. "What's wrong?"

"Nothing. It's nothing, really." She hiccuped back a sob and shook her head. "I'll manage."

His stomach dropped. "What will you manage?" *And why?*

"Another job I set up before the lottery draw just canceled. I've kept a few clients, but everyone believes that when I become a princess I won't work, so…" She laughed but there was no humor in the sound.

When I become a princess.

Those words shouldn't matter, but his heart wanted to cling to them.

"Royalty works all the time."

"I know. But not an actual job. I worked so hard on the floor of that tiny apartment and in the rented office I had. The life I'd planned for myself, the life that was supposed to keep me safe, that was supposed to build a life away from my family name—it's slipping through my fingers."

She sucked in a breath and pressed her hand to her chest. "It was my purpose. What I was good at. I can't draw or create beautiful dresses out of my imagination. I don't feel called to write or work in a glass studio. But I can see other's visions and I can make it a reality for them. Take their hopes and dreams and create the path to success for them. Princesses don't run businesses is all people can see."

"What if you did run it?" Alessio ran his hand along her back. "What if you had your marketing firm and the crown?"

"What?" Brie looked at him, her eyes bright with so many questions.

There was no reason she couldn't work. No law prevented a princess from running her own business. He should be telling her that she could end this experiment now, end the relationship, but he didn't want to let her go.

"I love you." The words danced from his mouth. "You are my other half. I never expected that. I don't know what you feel or…"

Brie's hand landed on his lips. "I love you, too. I'm not sure how it happened or when. But I love you, Alessio."

"What if we announce later this week that you plan to run your marketing business from one of the palace's office suites? It might not be as big an operation as you planned before. We'll still have royal duties, after all. But I guarantee you clients will flock to your inbox."

"You mean it?" Brie wrapped her arms around his waist, leaning her head against his shoulder.

"Yes. You are a royal, or you will be. But that doesn't mean you can't be your own person." It didn't. Not for her. He'd find a way to make that the truth.

"So if I wanted my first client to be a glass-worker whose art is magnificent…"

She could have a different life inside the gilded cage of the palace. He couldn't, but he wasn't going to argue that point now.

"Your first client will be Ophelia and she would definitely agree with me."

"She would." Brie laughed.

A knock echoed at his door.

Brie looked through the open door between their rooms. "Someone is looking for us."

"Jack. He has coffee, and a surprise for you."

"A surprise?"

"Yep. Do you want that or coffee more?" He winked, hoping the joke would make her smile.

It did.

"I always want coffee."

"Want or need?" Alessio grabbed her hand and pulled her through the door.

"Good morning, Your Royal Highness. I have coffee and—" Jack looked up from the coffee cart, pausing as he saw Brie standing next to Alessio. "Good morning, Ms. Ailiono."

"Brie, Jack. Just call me Brie."

Jack nodded, and Alessio watched Brie roll her eyes. The man's family had served royalty in European courts for more than a century. When they married, he'd call her Princess or Your Royal Highness. He was raised in old-school protocol and would never shift.

Jack stepped back out of the room, and Brie headed toward the coffee tray. She poured herself a cup, added two sugar cubes and a dash of milk, then took a deep sip.

Alessio watched her sink into the morning ritual, knowing it was grounding her. Coffee was a thing Brie claimed to live for, but he suspected it was really her liquid safety blanket. A routine she needed.

"All right, I have the dress here." Jack stepped back into the room, carrying a dress bag that he quickly hung on the door of Alessio's closet.

"Dress?" Brie's eyes flew from the bag to Alessio.

"For tonight, Ms. Ailiono." Jack stepped up to the dress, but Alessio waved him off.

This was his surprise. Maybe it was selfish, but he wanted to do the reveal. Jack took the hint, offered a quick bow and left them alone.

"I have a dress for tonight. A simple blue dress your mother found. She said it matched my eyes."

"And she wasn't wrong." Alessio stepped to

the dress bag. "But this one was made for you. I knew that the moment I saw it."

Brie raised a brow as she set her coffee cup down. "Saw it…"

He unzipped the bag.

Brie's breath hitched.

This was the moment he'd wanted. The realization. The understanding.

"The mermaid dress." Her hand was over her mouth.

"My mother is right—blue is lovely on you." He looked at her. Her eyes were so full of emotion, so full of love.

"It's over-the-top. I might get more press than King Sebastian." Brie giggled as she moved toward the dress.

"I suspect Sebastian would enjoy that. But in truth, it is his first state dinner. We are mere ornaments to this play."

Brie wrapped her arms around him, holding him. "You are always more than an ornament, Alessio. At least to me."

"That's more than enough."

That's more than enough.

Brie had replayed Alessio's words all day while she was prepped for the state dinner. Today was the first time she felt like she was truly acting the role of princess.

It was the role she'd play for the rest of her life.

And she'd get to keep her business, too. She would stand beside the man she loved and work the career she craved. Alessio was making dreams she'd never considered come true. She didn't mind being the lottery bride, helping the country, if she still got to be herself.

"Wow."

Alessio's voice echoed in her soul as she turned to look at him.

"You look—"

"Not like myself!" Brie's giggle was too high-pitched.

Her body was a work of art, but she was a ball of nerves. Tonight was the first night in the real role she'd play as Alessio's life partner. It needed to be perfect.

A beauty technician had worked on nearly every part of her today. Her toenails were bright blue in the peep-toe shoes. Her fingernails were a light green.

The makeup artist the palace had hired had looked at the dress and squealed with excitement. The woman had spent nearly an hour highlighting and contouring while palace staff went over protocols with her.

"You look mythical."

"Mythical."

She looked in the mirror one last time. Her hair wasn't wet. In fact the braid looked almost like a crown, though she wouldn't wear one of those until they were married.

Still, she looked like a mermaid. It was what the dress was designed to do. Ophelia was truly an artist.

"Protocol talked with you?"

Ad nauseam!

The woman had prefaced that this was King Sebastian's night so many times that Brie had almost asked if she and Alessio could just skip the thing altogether.

"Yes. I run a tight ship on the outings I plan, but when the palace is in control…" It was next level. Tonight was not about Brie and Alessio. That had been made clear. "I promise not to outshine King Sebastian."

The tips of his lips tilted down, and Brie wanted to yank her words back.

This was Alessio's lived experience. He'd grown up the spare, always walking behind his father and his brother. There was a protocol for who was highest in the family.

"I'm sorry." She stepped toward him, reaching for his hands.

"You don't need to apologize. I'm sure that is what the office said. Though perhaps more diplomatically."

"*Diplomatically* is cutting." The words were out before she could think them through. Again.

"I just mean…" She blew out a breath. If this

was a movie, she'd have a loose piece of hair to push out of her face or blow away. Instead, she was literal perfection. "Their words are very sweet. Controlled, yet…" She shrugged, not sure why she was trying to describe how listening to the protocol officer felt.

"Yet biting. A reminder that you aren't supposed to shine too brightly."

It was this attitude that had chased him to Scotland, but she was not going to let it happen around her.

"Alessio." She squeezed his hand. Today was the first time she'd heard the words *be smaller* since she stood by his side. Everything about her marketing campaign for the country was about blending into the background—but that was for a different purpose.

"Are you all right?" His fingers ran along her chin.

"Careful, you'll get glitter on yourself." She looked beautiful, but was it too much? Protocol had told her the lotto bride was taking a back seat this evening.

Lotto bride.

It was what she was and was the title she'd used with everyone before she and Alessio agreed to make it real. Now that their relationship was a fact, the tag felt like a slight.

And not just to her. But to Alessio.

"I don't care about some glitter." His thumb traced her jaw.

"I'm fine." It was true, but anger was overtaking the nerves she'd had all day. "But we need to find our own place after the wedding. We can still serve the throne, without actually living next to it. And I'll have my business to handle."

And he'd have his glasswork. He'd deflected her comment this morning, but she was going to find a way to get him regular time in his shop.

His eyes brightened and his smile made her want to strip the suit from his shoulders and spend the night luxuriating in the warmth it drove through her soul.

"I think that can be arranged, Princess."

A knock nearly made her jump. This was really happening.

"Ready, Your Royal Highness and Ms. Ailiono?" Jack's voice echoed from the other side of the door.

"Showtime." Alessio dropped his lips to hers.

They needed to get going, but Brie wrapped her arms around him, deepening the kiss. The world could wait a few moments longer. Alessio's hands stroked her lower back as she drank him in.

The glittery world she was about to step into was just for show. Her and Alessio, and the life they built away from the cameras, from the palace, from duty—that was reality. The reality she craved.

He broke the kiss as another knock came. "Duty awaits."

"So it does. Stay by me." Brie's skin felt slick as she wrapped an arm through his. She'd been in front of the cameras for weeks. There was no reason for tonight to feel different.

It did, though.

Because I love him.

"You are going to do great. I won't leave your side."

He'd be by her side. Brie could do this, and royal events would get easier...right? The shine would leave the lotto bride, but Brie was still enough. She was. *Right?*

She smiled and fell into step beside him. "I'm holding you to that, Prince Charming."

The room was warm—like all crowded events—but Alessio was hyperaware tonight. All eyes had flown to Brie when she stepped into the room. His heart had nearly exploded watching everyone's heads turn as she walked in.

Brie, his princess.

"Your fiancée is quite lovely." One of the ambassador's entourage smiled as he looked toward where Brie was talking to a few other dignitaries.

She looked over at him and nodded. He made sure that he was never more than a few feet from her.

"She is beautiful inside and out, and brilliant."

Brie was the most beautiful woman he'd ever seen. And her family had hoped to capitalize on that beauty by marrying her to a business associate. That was only one piece of her. One tiny, tiny piece.

Alessio loved every part of her.

"She will be the talk of this evening. The gown is something—a show." The man's words were cool, but Alessio heard the statement in them. Brie was the star.

That was a problem.

Sebastian was hosting. Sebastian was meant to be the focus.

"I am surprised she didn't post it on your social media page. It has been less active lately."

The man's gaze focused on Brie and the direction of the conversation gave him pause. It wasn't that it was less active; it was that there was less of him and Brie. It hadn't been conscious, at least he didn't think so, but as they grew closer, sharing private moments, kisses, felt off.

That was a worry for another day. Right now he needed to find a way to refocus the evening on his brother's success. This was Sebastian's event. Alessio nodded to the dignitary, his eyes moving subtly around the room.

He'd lost track of his brother.

Once, it had been Alessio ducking out of these events and Sebastian covering for him when he said something flippant. Since his return, Alessio had protected his brother, offering a response when Sebastian froze or said something glib.

His role was to support his brother, a role he wouldn't have yet if Alessio had stayed in Celiana. Still, Sebastian knew how to play this game. He'd been good at it, too. Once upon a time.

Heat flashed up his neck and Alessio took a deep breath. It wouldn't do any good for people to see his frustration.

Where was the king?

"Everyone will be talking about the princess tomorrow."

The words struck him, and he looked again for Sebastian, still not finding him. Would he be in one of Alessio's old hiding spaces or someplace new?

"And her dress! I've never seen such a creation."

The conversation floated over him as he kept looking over the crowd. Where was the king?

"Will you excuse me for a moment?" Alessio waited for the dignitaries to offer a polite response, looked toward Brie and was relieved to see she was fine. It was Sebastian he needed to find.

Alessio moved through the crowd, searching for the tall, dark-haired king. He should be easy to find.

"Alessio." His mother's voice was soft but urgent as she captured his arm.

He saw the same panic in her eyes that he was

feeling. Sebastian had slipped away. From his first state dinner. This was...this was a nightmare.

"Can you please tell the ambassador about Celiana's tourism goals? It's one of my youngest's pet projects." Queen Mother Genevieve smiled, but Alessio knew she was close to breaking.

"Pet project?" The ambassador raised a brow.

His mother had already wandered off. Alessio shrugged. "My mother downplays my interest a little."

It wasn't intentional. He just wasn't the king. As the heir, he helped, but there was no expectation that he'd sit on the throne. So his projects became "pet projects," even if they were literally the saving grace of the kingdom.

"My fiancée and I are heavily invested in ensuring Celiana's future." Alessio saw his mother disappear through a side door. "Let me tell you all we've accomplished."

"Where have you been?" Alessio strode to his brother's side as he saw him enter the ballroom from a side door.

"I had some business to attend to with the ambassador."

"Really?" Alessio wanted to shake him. The lie was preposterous, and Sebastian had to know that. "I've been with the ambassador for the last hour. He is interested in discussing trade options with parliament tomorrow."

"Then I wasn't really needed anyway, was I?" Sebastian nodded and started to walk off. "You and your bride-to-be had everything handled."

Brie.

Alessio's body went rigid. He'd been so focused on the ambassador and finding Sebastian, he'd wandered away from her. She'd been on her own for more than an hour now, all because he'd had to play the role that was meant to be Sebastian's.

"You're the king." Alessio's tone was harsh. "Act like it."

"Baby brother." Sebastian clicked his tongue. "What would our father say to that?"

It was a low blow. A consequence of boys who were close, at least once. They knew where to hurt each other. Which was why it was so easy to respond.

"What would he say about the man wearing the crown after him?"

Sebastian's face blanched but he didn't back down. "I suspect we'd both be disappointments."

The words were soft, but Alessio heard the hurt under them. He opened his mouth, but no words flowed.

"Enough of whatever this is," the queen mother said as she stepped toward them. "Sebastian, the ambassador is ready for dinner. And Alessio, Brie is handling herself well enough."

Well enough. Palace-speak for something was wrong, but they weren't going to speak of it here.

"This is Brie's first official function besides the day of the lottery. I think she's done exceptionally well." Alessio saw his mother's eyes widen. Since returning, he'd never pushed back. Never did anything more than fulfill his duty.

Which he'd done tonight to cover for the king's absence.

"Celiana comes first." The queen mother's words were tight. "You both need to remember that. Remember your father's expectations."

Sebastian made a noncommittal noise and wandered to the door leading to the dining room. A small bell rang, and the crowd turned to look at the king.

His father's expectations were the reason Alessio left…and the reason he was back.

"It is my pleasure to welcome Ambassador Ertel. If you will follow me, I know the staff has prepared a delicious dinner."

Alessio moved quickly to Brie's side. She linked her arm in his, but her face was devoid of the excitement he'd seen earlier. Her jaw was tense, her shoulders were tight and he was nearly certain that she'd rubbed some of the makeup off her face.

"Brie?"

"I'm fine."

The words were quick and an answer to a question he hadn't asked.

There were too many ears here, but as soon as he had her someplace more private, he was going to discover what had stolen the light from her eyes.

CHAPTER TEN

BRIE OPENED HER EYES, knowing there was still at least an hour before the sun rose. Alessio snored softly on the pillow next to her. They'd arrived back from the state dinner long after midnight.

Exhausted physically and mentally, she'd washed the remainder of her makeup off and they'd fallen into bed. Alessio had wrapped his arm around her, and she'd bit back her questions as he slipped into dream world.

The questions were pointless anyway. She knew the answers. That was the problem.

It was a problem the morning made even more difficult to ignore.

Slipping from the bed, she padded softly back to her room. She needed to get dressed, make coffee and settle her nerves.

He'd broken his promise last night. He'd left her. And the wolves had feasted.

Making it clear that the public might love the tourist uptick from the princess lottery but the aristocrats—the ones who'd spent a lot of money to try to make their daughters princesses—were not as pleased.

People had whispered, in just a loud enough tone to be overheard by her, about everything. How much makeup she was wearing—clearly too much. The dress she'd chosen—an obnoxious choice suited to her *social media*. The words were whispered with such viciousness they'd made her ill.

She'd not posted the dress or the process of getting ready. She'd thought of it, but it seemed too personal. Alessio had gifted her the dress because of their private time in Ophelia's shop. She'd wanted to hold to herself all the emotions that brought out. Perhaps that was a ridiculous statement for a princess.

More than one person had mentioned that she looked like she'd been trying to overshadow the king's event. The upstart lotto bride.

They insinuated she was stepping out of her sanctioned palace role to make herself and Alessio bigger, grander than they should be. Like she wanted to upstage the king.

And the king had disappeared…making her wonder if somehow, despite knowing how ridiculous it was, the words were true. Of course they weren't, but that didn't stop the pain of hearing them.

Her dress, the beautiful piece of artwork, was the talk of the event. She'd heard more than a few whispers and seen people with cameras snap a few shots when they thought she wasn't looking.

She'd been asked more than once if the palace had paid for the dress. She assumed the answer was yes, or perhaps Alessio had asked Ophelia to borrow it.

Then there'd been the not-so-subtle insinuations that she was nothing more than a stunt for the royal family. Those statements had flowed far too freely with Alessio's notable absence from her side.

Because of his absence.

The problem was that there was no way to deflect the "jokes," not when they were the truth. The fact that they'd fallen in love didn't change the fact that he'd pulled her name from a glass ball in a princess lottery that she'd joined as a marketing manager. That was the role she'd played for weeks now—blasting herself and Alessio across multiple social media platforms.

Without the princess lottery she'd still be in her tiny apartment, in comfy clothes, the rebel daughter of the Ailiono family. She'd have grown Ophelia's business, and her own, in a slower fashion. Hopefully.

The coldhearted truth of business was that success was not guaranteed, particularly when the most powerful business family in the country refused to talk to you. That meant she had a limited pool to prove success. More than half of new businesses collapsed within two years. Ophelia's was stable because of the lottery.

The reason everyone talked about Brie today was the lottery. And the words were less than kind when Alessio wasn't around to soften their tongues.

She left her room and headed for the media room. There was coffee there, and she needed to run some business plans past the few customers who'd stuck by her after her name was drawn. In a week or two she could tell them the plan for her to work as a princess. And there were videos to review of her and Alessio dancing last night that would work well for the social media campaign. With any luck one of them was relaxed enough for her to upload.

People had left more than a few comments that they wanted more of the prince and princess-to-be. A few weeks ago, Brie would have easily uploaded a playful kiss, or a video of them laughing. But as she grew closer to Alessio, those images—and she had many—felt too personal to give up for gossip.

She needed to do some marketing, though, a way to highlight the Ruins of Epiales they were visiting at the end of the week.

Turning the corner, she nearly ran into Jack. The man was flushed and holding several papers. A lifetime of reading body language made the hairs on the back of her head stand up.

"Ms. Ailiono."

"Jack." She watched him look at the papers then purposely away from her. "What's wrong?"

"Nothing." He was lying, trying to protect her.

"My brother always looked away when he was hiding something." At least he'd been that way when she'd seen him years ago. Perhaps now...

Focus, Brie.

"Ms. Ailiono." Jack's voice was so soft. But he didn't say any more.

"What's in the papers?" Brie crossed her arms.

"Alessio is still sleeping, so why don't you accompany me to the media room? I need coffee, then you can tell me what I did wrong last night."

Pink invaded his cheeks as he pursed his lips. The truth was radiating from him.

"You need to work on your tells, Jack."

He didn't offer a retort, but he did turn and follow her.

She entered the media room and immediately headed for the coffee bar. "I'll assume this is a 'strongest blend I have' kind of morning?"

"I suspect it is, Ms. Ailiono."

He waited as the pot brewed and she doctored the blend. Turning with the mug in her hand, she pointed at the papers that were still in his hand.

"What's the damage?"

Jack looked at his feet, then back at Brie. "The dress."

"Was lovely," Brie stated, hating that Alessio's gift, the mythical creation he'd chosen just for her, was causing problems.

"Yes." Jack moved to one of the tables and started laying out the papers. All online posts, from blogs, gossip sites...and finally the most reliable paper in the country.

Ailiono Family Taking over Palace!

Soon-to-Be Princess Spends over One Hundred Thousand to Outshine King!

Princess Briella—Royal Stunt Turned Royal Money Pit!

Jack had even printed the first slide of an online video breaking down Brie's sparkly makeup. It included commentary about how a princess did not sparkle, at least not more than the king. In one night, she'd gone from Alessio's beloved fiancée to an upstart.

The lottery bride turned villain.

Because of a dress.

It was ridiculous, but women had been torn down for so much less. A feel-good story earned hundreds of clicks, while a hit piece earned thousands, sometimes millions. As a marketeer she understood the dynamics.

As the focus of the stories, they stung. What would happen when they announced her plans to work outside the palace? Would that be seen as an upstart move?

She moved the papers and saw one other post under the others.

"Oh, I didn't mean to include—"

She read the headline.

Prince Alessio Already Tiring of His Lotto Bride?

The first paragraph of the article was direct.

Prince Alessio was noticeably absent from his fiancée's side last night. Our sources can confirm that the prince spent less than three minutes beside his future wife during the cocktail hour. One source remarked that Briella looked for him several times. No doubt she is learning that having her name drawn from a crystal ball does not actually make a princess.

The door to the library opened but Brie didn't look up. Tears coated her eyes, and she didn't want Alessio to see them. Today was already going to be hard. They needed a plan, a strategy to make sure that their plans for Celiana didn't unravel.

And to clear my name.

"Brie! I was hoping to—" His voice cut off, likely because he registered Jack in the room.

"Your Royal Highness. There were some reports about last night."

"The press noticed Sebastian's absence." Alessio's voice was tight. "I tried to cover."

"No." Brie wandered to the coffeepot, poured herself another cup and made one for Alessio, mostly to give herself something to do. To collect herself.

"The press didn't notice the king's absence."

Brie's fingers shook as she waited for Jack to finish his statement, to drop the hammer.

"The commentary is about Ms. Ailiono."

"Oh. Not Sebastian?"

"No. Not Sebastian." Brie's voice was tight as she turned to look at him. She knew he was his brother's keeper. Sebastian was the reason he was home, the one he felt responsible for.

But he'd given her his heart...or at least that was what he'd said.

"Brie..."

"The press is quite focused on the dress."

"I'm sorry. All of this is over a dress? I mean, that sounds like a win, considering what they could be printing."

"What!" Brie turned, pressing her hands behind her against the counter, mostly to keep herself in place.

Alessio raised his hand. "I just mean that if we have to choose between them running reports about a missing king or getting too focused on a dress, the choice is easy."

Brie walked to the table, grabbed the report about him tiring of her and one discussing how much she'd spent of the palace's coin. She marched toward him, slapped the papers against his chest, then left.

Rationally she knew that he'd not seen the articles. She knew he was reacting to what sounded like a silly idea. But he'd broken his promise. She'd been nervous. She'd asked him to stay by her side. If he'd been there...

This was what they'd printed over a dress. This

was just the beginning, and he was blowing it off to protect his brother. Because that was why he'd come home, why the rebel had become the dutiful.

But where did that leave Brie?

Prince Alessio was noticeably absent from his fiancée's side last night.

The first line of that article cratered his soul. He'd left her. That was true. The rest of it was absolute rubbish.

He wasn't tiring of Brie. The exact opposite. He looked forward to each moment, craved her touch. He loved her.

And the dress. He pushed his hand through his hair as he stepped into yet another room where Brie clearly wasn't. For a woman who'd rarely exited the media room over the last several weeks, she'd found a way to make herself remarkably scarce.

The dress was his gift. No citizen's funds had paid for it. Hell, Brie hadn't even planned to wear it. It was a surprise, his gift to her on what was her first true royal engagement—at least in her mind, even if the country never realized she'd planned to leave.

His surprise had blown up in their faces.

Another door, another empty room. Was she purposely hiding from him?

But what was he to do? If Alessio was honest,

there was nothing he could have changed about last night. Sebastian's absence was a bigger problem than a dress and observations about them not standing together in the hour before dinner officially started.

"Brother."

"Have you seen Brie?" The question was out before he'd even turned around.

"Good morning to you, too." His brother's brow furrowed as he moved toward him.

"I'm in no mood to play games, Sebastian. Have you seen Brie?"

"Not since last night."

"Do you even recall seeing her?" Alessio's tone was sharp, but he couldn't stop the frustration filling him. "After all, you weren't in attendance for a sizable portion of *your* event."

Color coated Sebastian's cheeks.

He'd aimed his words and they'd landed. His brother should have been there. It was his responsibility. Whether he wanted it or not.

"You covered well." Sebastian crossed his arms.

Righteous anger seemed to boil in his soul. He tried taking a deep breath but that did nothing to stop the fury. The man he'd been warred with the man he'd become after his father passed—and the first won.

"Where the hell were you?"

"I needed a break." Sebastian shrugged as though it was nothing.

"A break. A *break*!" Stars exploded in his eyes. What the hell?

Sebastian rocked on his heels but didn't step away. "Don't you ever need a break, brother? A break from the pressure pushing against your chest, shaking fingers, each breath more ragged than the next."

"Not since I returned." Alessio heard the deep wounds in his brother's description, and maybe if he knew where Brie was, if he knew she was all right, if he knew she hadn't left him, he might feel more understanding.

"Well, I don't have the benefit of getting to run away!"

Run away, pushed away, left for nothing until the crown wanted something of him. All those were words the man he'd been wanted to scream at Sebastian. But none of that was his brother's fault.

"You were born to be the king." They were their father's words, which Alessio had heard him state so often to his brother. They were whispered with as close to affection as their father got.

"What a prize." Sebastian looked at his feet, then back at Alessio. "If there was a path for abdication, the crown would be yours tomorrow. Then we'd see what you think of it." Then his brother turned on his heel and walked off.

"Sebastian!" Alessio understood the pressure. It wasn't the same for him, but he wasn't the person he wanted to be, either. Not anymore. At least he'd gotten a three-year reprieve. Sebastian would never get one.

"I'm sorry. I just need to find Brie. The press... I need to find her."

The king paused, and for a moment Alessio feared he wouldn't turn around.

"What did they say?" Sebastian started back toward him.

Rather than answer, Alessio held out the papers.

Sebastian read them, his brows rising at certain points. "These aren't nice, but—" He shrugged. "The palace's response is not to comment."

He knew that. The standard response was no response...unless it was about the king. The palace had squashed a few stories about their father, and more than one story about Sebastian's recent playboy lifestyle.

Alessio and Brie were not given the same treatment.

"I know. But Brie still needs comfort." She needed him this morning, and his mind had gone to where it always went since he returned home. The throne.

"Your bride is in the gardens. In tears," his mother said as she stepped from her rooms. Only her presence made him aware of where he was. He'd clearly been too focused on finding his fiancée to realize that he was so close to his mother's suite.

"Palace sources?" Sebastian sighed.

"Sources? Please, Sebastian. If you paid attention, gave anyone but the women you chase attention, people would tell you what you needed to hear, too." Genevieve had cultivated her staff well. She was their queen mother and employer, but she treated each member of the staff with absolute respect. It earned her their respect.

Alessio was trusted, too, but he was the spare, the one people bowed to but never paid as much attention to. It was the position he'd grown up in, the one he'd finally accepted when he came home.

"Which garden?" Alessio asked.

He didn't need to stay for whatever dressing-down his mother planned for his brother.

"Main courtyard."

"Thanks." He took off.

"No running in the halls."

He heard his mother's call but didn't slow his pace. He needed Brie.

Now.

He heard her sob before he saw her. She was sitting under a cherrywood tree, the stuffed animal Emilio had returned beside her. A set of notebooks was in front of her.

If she wasn't crying, the scene would be almost picture-perfect.

"Brie? Sweetheart?"

"Come to apologize?" Her voice wavered but the words were clearly a demand.

"Yes." He should have registered that she was upset, should have taken a few moments to comfort her before gently explaining that this was part of their role, too.

Sometimes he was the distraction—if it benefited the crown.

It was what he had to do. But by tying herself to him, she'd be expected to have the same role. The idea was a bitter pill as he slid to the ground, taking in her tearstained cheeks and red eyes.

"I'm so sorry, Brie."

She looked at him, her blue eyes still swimming with tears. Cocking an eyebrow, she raised her chin. "For...?"

"For not taking a moment to read the situation. For rushing to say that it was better that the press discusses a dress than Sebastian."

"Are you sorry for saying it, or sorry that it's true?"

"Brie—"

"I'm an Ailiono, whether my family wishes to claim me or not. I've been a sacrificial lamb before. How often will I have to do it here?"

Her words were daggers, sharpened weapons that struck with such precision.

"I don't know." Hiding that truth was not going to work.

"And what about when I'm working—will that be a host for gossip to redirect eyes from the palace?"

Working. Her company.

That was what this was really about, and there was more than a bit of jealousy in his chest that she'd asked about it. This wasn't really about them.

Maybe he should let her go, let her chase her dreams, relish the fact that he'd gotten more time than he deserved with a woman who made him feel whole.

The words to release her refused to appear. Instead, he said what was truly on his mind.

"You're my heart, Brie. All of it will work out. There will be hiccups and days that the barbs hurt. We just have to let the noise float away."

"Float away. Sticks and stones can break your bones, but words can never hurt you." She wrote something in the journal in front of her without looking at him.

"Words hurt. That schoolyard rhyme was made to make bullies feel better, not because it contains an ounce of truth." He leaned forward and put his hand on her knee. "Brie, look at me."

She raised her head. Shadows hovered under her eyes. She was clenching her teeth but there was a hint of something in her gaze. A hope.

"I can play games. I grew up in them." She held up a hand before he could say something to that sad statement.

"Some might even say that as a marketeer, I'm a professional game player, making people believe that they need something or that their life will be better with such and such product. It's a skill, and I am good at it."

"Brie…"

"What I will not accept is being second with you." Her bottom lip trembled. "With you, I need to be first. *Our* dreams and goals need to be first. I could have come with you last night. If the headlines were 'Prince Alessio and Briella Ailiono Taking Too Much of Ambassador's Time' or 'Spare and His Lotto Bride Stealing King's Show,' I'd shrug my shoulders."

She reached for his hand. It was warm as she squeezed him, grounding them in the garden.

"I spent my childhood as a pawn to my family's ambitions. I fell for you, Alessio. I want to be by your side, but we get to have our own dreams, too."

"We do. We do, Brie. I promise."

He should have pulled her with him last night. He should have stayed by her side. She was right; they could have talked to the ambassador together. The stories likely would have read exactly as she stated.

"We are a team. Promise."

"All right. Apology accepted." She pressed her lips to his. "Now we have to focus on the next problem."

"Next problem."

"Yep." She flipped the notebook around. "You were noticeably absent from my side."

"I read the article, Brie."

"Good. Then you know that in the first instance we had that wasn't controlled by us, you looked like you didn't want me. We'd posted less on my social media as…"

Her cheeks brightened.

He dropped a kiss to her lips. "As it became real?"

"Yeah." Brie ran her hand along his jaw. "So how do we shift the narrative back to the love-birds, without throwing your brother under the well-deserved bus?"

"What is this I hear that Briella will work when she puts on the crown?"

His mother's words weren't harsh, but he could hear the steel in them. He wasn't sure which of the queen mother's staff had overheard and passed on the conversation, but it hardly mattered.

Alessio looked to the media room. He'd only just patched things over. She was planning their next steps and he was getting her coffee. This wasn't the time for the conversation, but one rarely got exactly what they wanted behind the palace walls.

Brie would, though. Somehow, he'd find a way to give her the choices she needed and the dreams she deserved.

"Brie plans to run the marketing firm she had before all this. It won't be for profit, though she plans to complete the work for the companies that have already contracted her."

Brie had told him that the few companies who'd taken a risk on her, and stayed on following the lotto bride announcement, deserved her to finish what they'd contracted. After that, her focus would be on the tourism industry and nonprofits.

It was a brilliant idea. One that would endear her to the country even more.

"That is not a good idea."

"Mother—"

She held up her hand and Alessio bit his tongue.

"Maybe in a few months. But right now, after last night, it will look like she is seeking freedom from the palace."

Freedom.

The thing Brie had craved her entire life. The thing she deserved.

"I fail to see how working during our union is seeking freedom from the palace."

Except he knew how the optics would look. Rather than doing "royal" duties, Brie would focus on her company. He could argue that the nonprofit work was an excellent royal duty, but it was different. And different was not something the royal family sought out.

"She will have too many duties. Your father took on too much. If you had stepped up sooner..."

Her words trailed off, but Alessio knew the ending. *Your father might still be here.*

The queen mother looked at the day calendar she carried, despite the staff switching to phones and tablets years ago.

"I have to see to some things. Let Brie know it won't work, Alessio. Your brother needs your help. It's not fair to give her dreams that cannot be delivered."

His mother turned and glided down the hall, the sweep of her shoulders just a hair off. *What dreams had she given up for Celiana?* That was a question she'd never answer.

But Brie was going to get her dream. It might take him longer to figure it out. A delay was necessary. That was all.

Or I could set her free.

The thought rocked his soul. Maybe it was the right answer. She could still have her dreams, outside the palace, without the royal life holding her back.

Alessio looked to the door of the media room and shook his head. No. There was a way for her to have it all. Maybe just not right away.

CHAPTER ELEVEN

"HERE WE GO!"

Brie waved to the camera as Alessio held her close. It should feel nice, should be lovely. Maybe it would, if it felt real. When the camera was off, they did fine—sort of. Alessio had pulled away since the state dinner earlier this week. It felt like there was an answer he wasn't giving. Or maybe she just hadn't asked the right question.

No matter what she tried, it felt like there was a wall between them, and she had no idea how to strip it down.

"Will that one work?" Alessio's sigh echoed in the car as they pulled up to the Ruins of Epiales.

They hadn't had as many redo moments since the first week. Brie looked at the video and knew it wouldn't work. They looked like robots, not two people in love. It would just fuel the conversations already running wild.

"No." She bit her lip and kissed him. He softened in her arms. The two of them were becoming as close to one as possible in the back of the car. This was the moment they needed to capture, but she also hated sharing it when it felt like the only time they were close was when the camera wasn't an option.

"How about you do one as we head to the moors?"

She nodded, kissed him again, knowing that wouldn't be best but it was better than the video they had. She stepped out of the car and shivered.

The Ruins of Epiales always felt chilly to Brie. The old palace and fortress of Celiana had been built around the same year as the Roman Colosseum. It was in worse shape than the giant structure in Italy, but there were still identifiable walls and a sanctuary.

Epiales, the personification of nightmares according to the Greeks, wasn't worshipped here, but according to legend, the ruler of Celiana had dreamed of invasion in the year AD 300. It was a nightmare he hadn't believed until it had come true.

"We're at the Ruins of Epiales today!" Brie waved to the camera, then panned to the ruins, making sure to capture a shot of Alessio while avoiding the security detail that was always just far enough away to give the illusion of aloneness.

The ruins' historical records were minimal, though archaeologists agreed that the area had been ransacked and burned. The place certainly harbored nightmare energy, but whether anyone had experienced nightmares before the area was destroyed, no person walking the earth for generations had known.

"This is an impressive site." Brie turned the camera back to herself and tried to ignore the unease. It *was* an impressive site, but its vibes always felt off to her. It wasn't something Brie could put into words. "Into archaeology? Or hikes in

unique locations? Then this is the site for you."
Brie smiled, then shut off the video and hit Upload.

That would have to work.

Whatever the general dread of this place was, it felt stronger today. She ached to wrap her arms around herself as she and Alessio followed the guide.

She had to pull away from the creeping dread that had followed her since the day after the state dinner three days ago.

The seismic shift had rattled the very foundation of her soul.

A week ago, she'd have stepped into Alessio's arms, walked hand in hand with him, joked about the icky feeling this place gave her or made some silly, or spicy, joke to lighten the creepy mood of the ruins.

Now, though...

She looked ahead. He was only a foot or so in front of her. Brie could reach her hand out and touch him. The small physical distance was highlighting the chasm she felt growing between them.

The worst part was that Brie knew she should do it. That was the plan they'd hammered out in the garden: ignore the press and be as they were. She should reach for him, make the jokes, put the smile on. Play the game. After all, the papers were already running wild with speculation that the lottery stunt was coming to an end.

And once more the papers were focused on one

thing. The mermaid dress was old news. Now all the press could talk about was the lack of a ring on her engagement finger.

Even now she absently rubbed the empty finger. Alessio had offered her a choice of rings when they'd started this stunt, but she'd not wanted one. Somehow that would have made this real.

Now that it was real, now that everyone was noticing, Brie couldn't help but feel the slight even if Alessio hadn't meant anything by leaving her without an engagement ring. In fact they'd discussed it last night. And he'd worried how it would look if they chose one while all of this was going on.

He was right.

But he'd also recommended holding off on announcing that she'd be keeping her marketing firm. Just until this blew over. There was no need to spin up more scandal.

They were the right words, too. She knew that, knew that it would be more illustration that their relationship was nothing more than a glorified marketing campaign for the country.

The irony that this was how it had started was far from lost on her.

Still, it felt like there was more to the story. There was something he wasn't telling her. Or maybe she was looking for cracks. Whatever it was, they weren't the same as they'd been.

And everyone was noticing. They'd not been acting before, not trying to tell a story. It had come naturally, a gift she'd not recognized until it was gone.

Now they needed to tell the story. They needed to quash the rumors, the cutting looks, the whispers. Now was the time to play the role of prince and future princess.

And it should be such an easy story to tell. They didn't have to pretend.

"This place is glorious." Alessio breathed in as they stepped to another section of the ruins. "Sad, but glorious."

"Yes." Brie nodded, happy to have some conversation other than the thoughts her mind was supplying.

"You can envision how beautiful it must have been just after it was completed." Her words were right, but they felt off. Stiff. Like she was talking to a tourist rather than the man she loved.

Alessio moved, and for a moment she thought he was reaching for her, looking for her hand.

But before he connected, the tour guide stated, "If you close your eyes, you might even feel the spirits."

Alessio turned and a chill slipped down Brie's back. As a rule she didn't put much credence in ghosts. However, she never quite ruled them out, either.

It would be nice to pretend it was the ghouls sending cool air racing across her skin, rather than the empty feeling of watching Alessio stuff his hands back in his pockets as he followed the guide's instructions.

Closing his eyes, he stood perfectly still. The wind blew his hair, and Brie drank him in. He was gorgeous, though the wear of the last few days was visible, too.

The lines around his eyes, the hint of darkness under them and the pinch of his jaw... The image he showed the world of the relaxed, dutiful prince was absent.

At least to her knowledgeable eyes.

Neither of them were sleeping well.

Her brain refused to turn off. It kept replaying the horrid headlines that graced websites and the few printed papers still around. It whispered terrible things, usually in the sound of her mother's voice.

She'd gone from the lotto princess bride to the interloper in one night. With one dress.

And the palace had said nothing. Alessio had said nothing. They didn't want to throw the king under the bus, though Brie wouldn't have minded doing it.

But couldn't Alessio have said that he bought her the dress as a gift? Couldn't they have issued some joint statement, been a team united instead of the quiet pair they'd become?

Their silence just fueled the questions she now heard peppered through crowds meeting them. The frowns she saw were difficult to ignore. And they seemed to chase slumber away.

As a result, Alessio was constantly shifting with her movements. She'd even mentioned moving back to her bed if her tossing was keeping him up. He'd declined each offer. That warmed her heart. He wanted her in his bed.

But that didn't chase the worries away that he was hiding something.

"I don't feel anything." He opened his eyes and grinned.

"Really?" Brie found that difficult to believe. Maybe he didn't feel ghosts, but the air felt... heavy, like the general vibe between them. There were so many things to feel.

"Do you?"

"I feel cold." The words came out before she could think them through. She bit her lip and tried to force a smile, tried to make things feel normal between them.

"The wind off the ocean is a bit biting."

Alessio tilted his head and looked at their guide, who'd given them a little space. It wasn't a lot, not enough privacy that they could have a real conversation. And the Ruins of Epiales were not the right place anyway.

He stepped closer and she waited for his arms to wrap around her. She waited to be pulled close... but the moment didn't come.

"We can leave. The press got a few pictures of us arriving, you put up the video and this is prob-

ably a pretty niche tourist location. Not sure anyone is visiting Celiana just for this place."

The ruins were interesting, if you were already
on the island, but tourists seeking these kinds of
places had far more exceptional locations to visit.

"Do you want to leave?" She buried her hands
in her pockets. If he wasn't reaching for her, then
she wouldn't reach for him.

"Brie—" Alessio shifted, opening his mouth
and closing it before saying whatever was on his
mind.

Then looked back at their guide. "The princess
is a little chilly. I think we're going to cut this outing a bit short."

"Of course." The guide nodded, but Brie saw
the hint of something in his eyes—a note of glee,
or excitement. It was wiped away by a soft smile
so fast she was sure she'd misread it.

Stop looking for worries, Brie!

If only her brain would listen.

The guide started back down the path to where
their car was waiting. Alessio looked at her, his
jade eyes seeming to bore into her soul, then he
stepped to the side and started down the hill after
the guide.

She sucked back a sob. Something needed to
shift, needed to change; they couldn't continue
like this. But what if asking the questions shattered her heart?

What if it's already shattered?

Brie looked out at the ruins one last time. The once beautiful location had been worn away by time and fire. She wrapped her arms around herself, then straightened her shoulders.

She was in charge of her life. That hadn't changed just because she'd fallen in love with Prince Alessio.

Turning, she followed the path Alessio had taken. Had he even noticed that she wasn't right behind him?

Alessio stared at the empty path and tried to determine if he needed to go after Brie. Or would that make the already uncomfortable divide between them larger?

He'd thought she was right behind him. After all, she'd said she was cold.

And rather than pull her close, I said we should leave.

Because pulling her close felt off, like it was for show. Behind closed doors they were better than in public, but not as good as they'd been. She'd agreed to delay announcing her plans to work, and he hated that he hadn't told her what his mother had said.

Alessio felt like he was acting. He felt like everything was for a show he no longer wanted to star in. He wanted Brie, not the drama, not the pain he suspected the palace would inflict on her someday.